Thank you, Jennifer,

Blessings on you!

Rick Elliott

Faith Journeys
of the Heart

Rev. Rick Elliott

Faith Journeys
of the Heart

Tate Publishing & Enterprises

Faith Journeys of the Heart
Copyright © 2008 by Rev. Rick Elliott. All rights reserved.

Published by Tate Publishing & Enterprises, LLC
127 E. Trade Center Terrace | Mustang, Oklahoma 73064 USA
1.888.361.9473 | www.tatepublishing.com

Tate Publishing is committed to excellence in the publishing industry. The company reflects the philosophy established by the founders, based on Psalm 68:11,
"The Lord gave the word and great was the company of those who published it."

Book design copyright © 2008 by Tate Publishing, LLC. All rights reserved.
Cover and Interior design by Stefanie Rooney

Published in the United States of America

ISBN: 978-1-60696-886-4
1. fiction, general
08.11.03

Dedication

In memory of *Eve Elliott*, my mother,
and
In honor of *Rusty Miller*, my surrogate mother.
You helped me maintain my inner child's creativity.
Special thanks to the people of my various parishes
whose responses helped me hone my craft,
and to *Barbara Robidoux* for her skillful editing.

Table of Contents

Foreword

Emily Dickinson, in one of her more delectable turns of phrase, said, "Tell all the truth you can, but tell it slant." The stories you are about to read are more often than not tales of a slanted truth. Rick Elliott is a preacher by profession, as am I, and we preachers are too often known as purveyors of obvious truths, horizontal truths, in-your-face, my way or the highway truths. It is little wonder that we have been the butt of no end of pilloried assault as possessors of small minds, thus proclaimers of small and trivial truths.

Why not tell stories, then? Why not offer the stuff of real life, the grit of genuine experience the better to combat the dangers of so-called universals? In the stories of our lives, there is no experience that is just like yours. I really do not know exactly how you feel, because you are you and I am I, and I need to be satisfied with that. To listen carefully to your life is to learn something of you and to learn something for myself—but hardly all I need. Stories, it has been said, give me practice for my living.

But even that does not capture the delight of the reading of a story. A story creates its own world, another world, an alternative reality, thus opening up worlds unimagined before my reading. That great American theologian, Mark Twain, once opined, "Familiarity breeds contempt—and children." He was, of course, right in both instances, but familiarity breeds far more than contempt. It breeds indifference, laziness, and boredom. A story opens a window onto a fresh landscape, a new horizon, another kind of seeing and feeling.

Rick Elliott opens such windows for us, taking the old truths and making them new. But not just new. Different, fresher, richer, truer. So read these little nuggets, these slanted truths, these sharper vistas of the world in which we live. And feel with new power the truth that lies deep down, but is too often obscured by the obvious, the mundane, the trivial. Here is a preacher who preaches in stories. Not so far from that other preacher so long ago who always seemed to have a story at hand when something new needed saying.

John C. Holbert
Lois Craddock Perkins Professor of Homiletics
Perkins School of Theology

Introduction

Early in my ministry I had a nagging feeling that I wasn't getting all I could get from a Scripture passage using the traditional exegetical skills I'd been well taught in seminary. After a while, I discovered that each passage had something in common; each had emotion as a significant component. I had started writing short stories at the University of North Carolina at Chapel Hill and wrote one for a seminary project. So I decided that writing stories might be a way of involving people in the emotion of a passage.

I Believe in God the Father was my first attempt. It met with much appreciation by the congregation I was serving. *Pro Bono Publico* started as a story I wrote at Chapel Hill. I realized that it fit one passage quite nicely. So I reworked it. Most of the stories began their journey as sermons I preached where I was serving. Turning them from an aural audience to a reading audience proved quite a challenge.

It is my fervent wish that these stories will lead you on your own *Faith Journeys of the Heart*.

Rick Elliott
Houston, Texas

Return Engagement

You could call it a return engagement, though it certainly wasn't planned as one. In fact, it was a total surprise. Bob was driving down the interstate highway, struggling to see through the heavy rain that drenched the windshield almost faster than the wipers could sweep it off. His world had narrowed itself to a small tunnel that appeared intermittently between the swish-swipe of the blades. There was no time dimension, no space, just a narrow world bounded by rain, fog, the windshield, and his state of mind.

Road signs along the way related progress being made—one heralded a town so many miles off, then another would tell when that town was being passed. Bob was aware enough of the dashboard gauges to stop when gas was needed. But even that task dissolved into the narrow world in which he existed. Other people were traveling on this road, passing by in trucks and

13

cars, but Bob paid them no mind. They were outside of the tunnel into which his world had compressed.

A brief lull in the downpour broke the spell. It was 2:30 in the afternoon, though it looked more like twilight. Some primordial-like force lured Bob off the highway and toward a small, county-seat town in Central Alabama. Only then did he realize he was ravenously hungry.

It wasn't until he found himself on a small highway that he realized where he was going. "It was the main highway, two highways ago," Mrs. Moody had told them. "There used to be a lot of traffic by here goin' between Montgomery and Mobile."

Bob smiled when he came upon a propped up mileage sign riddled with buckshot. A stranger could tell Montgomery was ahead, but there was no way of knowing how far ahead. Even though he'd only been in this area once before, Bob had no trouble knowing where he was. Little sights along the way seemed as familiar to him as streets traveled every day of his life. The goal was near. A knot that had been in his stomach for several days began to unsnarl—and the "feed me" burbles quieted as if they knew food were near at hand.

And there it was—*Moody's Steak House!*

Bob pulled into the sparse gravel parking lot. The place was even more disheveled than it had been when he and Barbara had stopped there on one of the most memorable trips they'd ever taken together. All of the neon letters were glowing, but some were beginning to fade. The white stucco on the front of the building was crackling; the barn-red paint on the steps and trim was flaking.

One set of steps led to what looked like a place where a family might have lived. The building was boarded up. Bob hoped it was because the business had done well enough that nicer quarters—someplace else—had been purchased. The center steps moved up from two sides to a covered platform. Then more worn, red steps led from the platform to the front door. Bob caught himself struggling up the steps, but what crippled him was a memory. "That was a year ago," he reminded himself out loud.

Time seemed to collapse as if Barbara were still struggling up those steps on her own. Then, with an impish smile, she had extended a slim, Band-Aid-covered hand for help. Though, by then, more than a hand had been needed. He almost had to lift her up each step, clutching her tightly under her arms.

On a whim Bob bypassed the memory and turned to see if the bumper-sticker window was still there. He'd had a few seconds as he waited for Barbara to ask for help back then. She insisted on asking first. So he'd looked at the fascinating crazy quilt of bumper stickers festooning a window, sometimes several layers thick. One particular batch caught his eye. They'd just been slapped up there, so bits and snatches of stickers could be seen underneath. The top bumper sticker touted George Wallace. Underneath George was a sticker just visible enough to realize it was for John Kennedy. And underneath JFK was Stevenson. Then

Dixiecrat Strom Thurmond. Bob had fancied that underneath them all was one for Franklin Roosevelt. They were a testimony in their illogic to the politics that had predominated throughout a broad swath of the United States.

When Barbara had finally made it up the steps and opened the door, they were greeted by a gray-haired sprite. Her shoulders hunched up some around her neck, and she had the beginnings of a *widow's hump*. She was dressed in a wild, floral-print, happy coat, black slacks, and black Reeboks which seemed almost to swallow her feet and ankles. Astounding figure though she was, her eyes were what caught Bob's attention. They sparkled and danced as she greeted us. It was obvious Barbara was having a difficult time, but the sprite made seating them at the nearest table seem the most natural and normal thing to do.

With certain firmness to her voice (which genteelly implied she was to be heeded), she recommended that her guests choose from the dinner specials. Suddenly Bob realized they were the only people in the place; after all, it was past eight on Halloween night. Part of the charm of the run-down place was the steady stream of miniature ghosts, goblins, and fairies who paraded in and out as the couple dined. Each one got Mrs. Moody's undivided attention, topped off by a big, waxed paper-wrapped, homemade brownie.

Barbara and Bob had a hard time choosing from one of the several, mouth-watering, Southern-country entrees. Finally he settled on chopped steak, though the fried chicken sounded awfully good. Barbara chose the chicken. "That cook in the back looks like she really knows how to fry it up," she said. A tasty salad and homemade soup arrived quickly, then the entree, squeezed in amongst mounds of greens, corn, and mashed potatoes—all spiced with story after story from Mrs. Moody. She regaled the couple with tales of famous people who'd stopped there as they traveled between Mobile and Montgomery. She talked about Truman Capote stopping there once.

"That story he wrote about Christmas and his friend who wasn't all there—that wasn't too *fah* from here. And Tallulah Bankhead was here once. She came with a group of people who just opened the door and sorta took over the whole place.

"You know," she said, conspiratorially changing to a stage whisper, "she was a lot prettier in the movies than she was in person. And Doris Day. Did you know she had a face full of freckles? I wonder why we couldn't see them on the screen.

"And oh," she said, making a sashaying motion with a delicate lace handkerchief she found tucked under her watch, "President Kennedy was by here, too. But he wasn't president yet. He was campaignin' through here. My, he was a handsome man. He'd look at you and a lady's heart would just go a flutterin'." She tucked the handkerchief back in its safe, but accessible place.

As Bob looked back, he didn't recall her telling a single story about anything that took place after 1968, yet it was 1990 when they had been there.

When Barbara took a break from eating to try to let her dinner settle to make room for more delectable mouthfuls, she choked back a giggle and murmured delightedly, "Look, Honey, At those portraits of George and Lurleen Wallace!"

Bob didn't know how he'd missed seeing them before; they covered one whole wall, bigger than life. George exuded his bantam rooster energy and Lurleen was calmly smiling up at him.

Mrs. Moody changed course in her storytelling to relate how her husband had been the county campaign manager for George Wallace. "There's a park across the street, and that's where they used to hold the rallies," she told them. "Mr. Moody used to fry up a mess of catfish and feed all comers for free. George used to speak to me very respectful-like, so I guess that's why Mr. Moody helped him out on the campaigns." Then she giggled. "Neither one of us understood a gol-darned thing he talked about. He sorta hypnotized you into liking him."

It was clear that racism had no part in her life. She treated the rainbow stream of trick-or-treaters as if each one were her own child.

After they were all but bulging with food, Mrs. Moody surprised them with the most succulent-looking coconut crème pie they'd ever seen. Barbara and Bob devoured it. Afterwards, they had to slump back in their chairs because their stuffed stomachs wouldn't let their bodies bend so well in the middle. By that time the whole staff had gathered around the table.

They didn't seem to want their guests to leave. The couple had become that eagerly awaited company who finally has to go home.

Then Mrs. Moody brought a pie tin with two huge pieces of pie to the table. "I cain't serve it tomorrow," she announced with a grin. "It'll be stale. Thought you might want a midnight snack."

Bob turned the bill over to see what he owed—$4 each, tax included.

He and Barbara had talked about the dinner and the warm nest they'd fallen into all the way back to the motel. They almost forgot the laundry they'd started in the laundromat. When they went back for the clothes, they found that some good elf had neatly folded the laundry and placed it in the hamper they'd left there.

The pie wasn't eaten that night, but it sure was gobbled down the next morning along with some strong coffee. Many nice things happened on that trip, but whenever people asked about their adventures, Bob would always begin with Moody's Steak House and seldom described any further.

On this "return engagement." When he got to Moody's, he stopped to stare at the old bumper-stickers, imagining what the place might have looked like back then when this was the "real road between Mobile and Montgomery." He wondered why he had just struggled up those steps so laboriously when he didn't need to. Then he opened the door—and there she stood in the same wild, floral-print happy coat. The shoes were white Reeboks now. She was even more hunched over, her shoulders and ears almost touching. She was a little more stooped, too. But still her eyes sparkled and danced.

"You're that Okie preacher man, aren't you?" she asked.

"You remembered me!" Bob was astonished and strangely warmed.

"But someone's missin'."

He avoided her question and she let herself be diverted to other topics. Meanwhile the menu grabbed Bob's attention. At this point he could have eaten one of those old bumper stickers on the window outside. The chopped steak was listed there, like the last time. And the fried chicken Barbara had talked about and devoured. But now and again, Mrs. Moody would return to her puzzled statement: "There was someone with you." Bob ignored her.

There was smothered steak, too—that hadn't been on the previous menu. Again questions from Ms. Moody, which he brushed away as best he could. Forcing concentration on the typed menu with the cockeyed "e"—Bob pondered over the choice of vegetables. Mashed potatoes—yes, that would have to be included. Turnip greens—gra-eens they used to call them in East Texas. Fried okry—yes, it was really spelled like that. And more questions. His eyes wandered hopefully down to the desserts. Yes, coconut crème pie was there! But so was blackberry cobbler. Bob smiled as he remembered being a youngster at camp and picking wild blackberries. How great the taste of the cobbler was that the camp cook had made. She made it more like dumplings swimming in a sea of blackberries and juice.

Apple, cherry, and lemon meringue pies completed the list. Bob was on the verge of choosing two pieces of pie and having bites of each. And more questions.

Then Ms. Moody affirmed with a nod of her head, "I remember now. She was a proud woman who stood as erect as she could. She had a hard time walkin' and wobbled a lot. And her arms, they must have hurt a lot with all those sores."

Bob could evade it no longer. "She's dead," he announced. "I'm going to North Carolina to bury her." Then he broke. All the sadness he'd tamped down for days suddenly welled up in him all at once. The woman's soft hand patted his arm as she made gentle clucking sounds—the ones that can be uttered only at such a time.

As the worst of the sobbing began to ebb, Bob felt bony arms holding him tight, almost gently rocking him. "She was a real lady, wasn't she!" the woman whispered. Bob nodded agreement.

When he opened his eyes, it wasn't normal vision that was there, but some extra-dimensional sight through which he began to see all those who'd cared for and nurtured him through this tragedy. Somehow, he hadn't realized they were there until now. In the extra dimension he could see the woman with the rum cake who'd stopped by just as he had found Barbara dead. He could feel the hugs, hear the phone calls, remember the small needs of life which appeared to be taken care of on their own. And, most of all, he saw the caring faces of those people he'd come to know so well in such a short time. Moody Steak House became strangely filled with people who'd been with him all along, yet only now, had he seen them.

So with red eyes, and another piece of coconut crème pie "for a late-night snack," Bob walked out of Moody Steak House with the Body of Christ made known by everyday people as they supported him in his sadness and loss. Somehow he knew he'd been led there on this journey by Christ, who said, "Come to me all of you who are tired from carrying heavy loads, and I will give you rest" (Matthew 11:28, TEV).

When he got back into the car, he turned to where Barbara would have been sitting and said, half in fun, "Want a bite of Mrs. Moody's coconut crème pie?"

To this day and for always, he believes he heard her reply, "No, I couldn't eat another bite."

Christ is like a single body, which has many parts; it is still one body, even though it is made up of different parts...If one part of the body suffers, all the other parts suffer with it...All of you are Christ's body and each one a part of it.

1 Corinthians 12:12.26–7 (TEV)

He [God] will cover you with his wings; you will be safe in his care. God's faithfulness will protect and defend you,

Psalm 91:4 (TEV)

The Rebuke

Two mottled splotches of green caught Jeff's eye as he first walked by—some kind of mold or lichen. He'd never bothered to learn which during high school biology class. These growths differed from the usual splashes of green that thrive in moist areas protected from direct sunlight. These had formed a mascara-like accent on a faux marble statue. Cherub-chubby and innocent looking, the statue was set apart from its genre by the fountain attached to it. Water would usually pour from the mouth of this type of fountain. But this angel had water trickling from each eye, leaving a residue of green that looked like the grains of salt left on a face after crying. The statue had become an item of interest. Jeff looked forward to seeing it every morning and evening as he walked to and from the bus stop.

One evening, as he returned from work, Jeff noticed someone sitting by the fountain—a young man on the precipice of adulthood, leaping forward, yet still grabbing onto the security of childhood. He was tall and gangly, face dotted with pimples, clothes a rumple of things probably picked up from the floor of his room where they'd been deposited the night before. A gentle grace about his movements gave an inkling of what would probably come as he matured. He was crying. His narrow shoulders heaved from time to time as a throe of sorrow rippled through his body.

Jeff watched for some time, wondering whether or not he should approach. That internal war finally resolved, and he decided to try to lend some comfort. As Jeff approached, the lad took on the look of a deer caught in the headlights of a car. But that moment passed, and soon he was telling his story.

"I come here a lot," he said. "I love this crying angel because I cry a lot, too. I just don't fit in with the rest of the kids. I'm different. I got a bad grade in PE because I'm always late. I don't want to be in the locker room when the other guys are there. I wait until they've gone before I go in.

"Mom is inside the church talking with the minister. She's really mad at him because of what happened last night at the supper." He shook his head in amazement. "I don't know why I'm telling you all this, Mister, but I need to tell somebody. I tried talking to the pastor," a shrug of his shoulders, indicating a general direction, "but look at what *that* got me!"

Jeff waited as the boy tried to control more tears. Then he went on.

He told this horrible joke right in front of everybody. Something about gays and flower arranging. He thought it was hilarious. Mom didn't! She stood up, right there in front of all the people, and told him the joke was in poor taste and not appropriate for any place where loving Christians are gathered in fellowship. "It's demeaning!" she told him.

"Then the preacher said it! I still can't believe he did. He said, 'Well, what could we expect from you and your faggot son.'

"Faggot! That's what he called me. The only way he knew was because I had talked to him about some feelings I have that I don't understand. You won't make fun of me, too, will you?"

Jeff was hooked! What could have possibly possessed a man of God to say anything like that, particularly in public? As he embraced the sobbing child, Jeff became bound and determined that something needed to be done to nurture and heal this crushed young man.

Shortly, the mother came out of the church. Her face was red, the veins in her neck bulged. As she came toward them, her shoes tapped out a firm, purposeful rhythm. She was a force to be dealt with.

"Who are you?" she challenged.

He started to explain, but her son beat the words Jeff was forming. "He's okay, Mom, he's listening. He's okay."

"I'm angry about what happened," Jeff told her. "This is terrible. I'm an officer of another church of this denomination and something needs to be done about this! There are procedures that can be taken. At the very least, this clergyman should be admonished for what he's done and for the pain he's put you two through."

Marie introduced herself and her son, John. Jeff invited them to share an early supper. His wife, Kathy, was quick to take folks in, so Jeff knew it would be okay to bring these strangers home. Sure enough! There was more than plenty—even enough for a young man who was eating like he needed to feed two bodies. During the meal, the details came out in bits and snatches. Kathy was even angrier than her husband. After dessert, the four of them set down to work. An hour or so later they had mapped out a plan. Jeff was to talk to his minister to bone up on church law. Marie was to make an appointment with the area church executive. Kathy was going to hold down the home front. And John promised to keep a stiff upper lip at school.

The next day, first thing, Jeff called Pastor Esther and made an appointment for later that afternoon. It was an appointment Jeff would not keep!

Kathy called him at work, something she never did unless it was an emergency. His nerves were on edge before he picked up the receiver to hear what she had to tell him.

"Marie just called," she reported. "John's in the emergency room. He got beaten up at school."

"I'll meet you there in fifteen minutes."

When Jeff got to the hospital, Kathy was waiting for him. She had found out which ER cubicle John was in, so they ignored the efforts of a clerk to see whether or not they were family, and tore right through the doors. The doctor was stitching up John's arms and his head. But the worst wound was the pink smudge of a letter emblazoned on his forehead—a pink letter "F." Physical wounds were minor, fixable with stitches and time to heal. John's other wounds might never heal. The principal of the school was added to Jeff's list of people to see.

The next morning, before the bell rang for the first class, Jeff was seated in the man's office, describing what had happened on school grounds. The principal's face was a mask—a neutral façade that hid any feelings he might have had one way or the other.

"We'll look into this," he said in a tone that made Jeff realize nothing would be done about it. "They have these fights—the boys do—at this age. Their hormones take over and overrule the sensible parts of their brains. Yup, these fights happen, and we can't always be there when they do."

"But this is more than a fight," Jeff protested.

The man reassured him the matter would be looked into, and he'd be the first one to know when the appropriate parties had been disciplined.

The next week Marie asked Jeff to go with her to

see the denominational area executive. He and Kathy had been seeing her and John daily. He was losing weight and had a vacant look in his eyes. The kids were giving him a hard time; it was written all over his face.

The church executive listened with lots of sympathy. His appropriate words and gestures indicated he felt for John and his plight. "The church has ways of dealing with things like this," he told them. "All wrongs will be righted, but it's going to take time." In fact, he said that phrase so many times during their visit it became a kind of litany.

Pastor Esther called Jeff shortly after he got home. They made a date to meet later that day. It seemed the executive had called her right after they had left to find out details about her "friend with the attitude." When they met, Esther offered suggestions and encouragement. "The process will work," she assured. It was obvious she was fighting to be factual and issue oriented. Finally, she threw the book she'd been researching on the floor. Tears of anger welled in her eyes. "I'm so mad I'd throttle that pastor if he were here."

So they waited, and waited, and waited. Jeff tried to fill the father role for John whose dad had left years before, for parts unknown. Marie was raising her son by herself, and was managing well. Her gentle focus was on John. Once they were driving along and saw a dog that had been hit by a car. John insisted Jeff stop and take the dog to the emergency vet. He cradled the wounded animal in his lap all the way, getting blood and body fluids all over his favorite shirt.

And they waited.

Marie was getting anonymous, taunting calls. John had a range of mysterious diseases that were just serious enough for him to miss school, but not serious enough for him to go to the doctor.

And they waited.

Then Esther called. "Nothing's going to happen," she reported. "The investigating team is going to deep-six it. They'll wrap it up in so much red tape nothing will happen. They hope we'll all forget about it." The flatness of her voice indicated her defeat, disappointment, and bewilderment.

A month later she invited Marie to attend a women's conference with her. It was supposed to be special, and she thought Marie would enjoy it. John stayed with Kathy and Jeff. A room was fixed up for the visitor. Movies were rented. A trip to Six Flags was scheduled. They had a great time!

Marie returned refreshed and happy. The worry lines around her eyes had relaxed. She laughed heartily at Jeff's jokes, whereas before she'd just tittered politely. "We told everybody our story," she related. "They were appalled."

"I've made up my mind about something," Pastor Esther said. "I can't tell you now what I'm about, but let's just see if I can use some of my clout to get this investigation process out in the open. I've got some markers to call in with the exec. Let's see what I can do."

But those markers apparently weren't enough. Weeks continued to go by, then months. Nothing happened. Life at Marie and John's house had a fortress-like quality. Scarcely a weekend would pass without it being "rolled." Toilet paper stayed in the upper limbs of the trees and became a fluttering mass like Spanish moss, which was always there. The pink "F" was constant. Their front door had to be repainted so many times they finally decided to have it replaced with a metal one that wouldn't absorb paint. They changed their telephone number and paid extra to have it unlisted. But still a few sick souls ferreted it out so they could pour out their obscenities. Marie thought about moving, but she had lived in this city all her life—as had her parents and their parents, for four generations. She'd inherited the house, and doubted she'd ever be able to scrape up enough money to make a new start someplace else.

⤔

Then came the day to remember. The national assembly of the denomination was meeting in the capitol of a neighboring state. Marie and Jeff took a vacation day to attend. Esther broadly hinted they should do so.

The delegates were settling in for the first day of deliberations, seated in theater rows facing a dais and podium. A murmur rippled through the crowd, and people began to talk in small groups as Pastor

Esther was moving around in the delegate area. As the meeting began, a regal, older woman stood in place and demanded to be recognized. "Will the moderator please tell us about this letter?" she called out.

A chorus of voices echoed her request. "Yes, we want to know, too."

The moderator looked bewildered as he turned back and forth, consulting various support staff for advice. "I'll refer this matter to the national clerk," he finally announced.

The clerk looked just as bewildered. Then Pastor Esther strode to the front and presented him with a copy of the letter. Purposefully she strode back to the visitors' area and began to pass out copies of the letter to the crowd. Jeff couldn't believe what it said. It was addressed to the delegates and titled, *A True Story*. No names or places were revealed, but it was John's story—and Marie's—one that sought justice from this august body.

The national clerk read and re-read the letter. Finally he said, "I can't see how this body can act on this. Due process will have to be followed in the regional body before it can be dealt with nationally."

So the matter was passed on to the regional body. Maybe now something would happen—now that it was all out in the open. The delegates cornered Pastor Esther during a break. Several wanted more details. Who was it? Where did this happen? But Esther would say nothing more than what was on the printed page.

But the executive knew. And John and Marie's former pastor would soon know, too.

By this time, John and Marie had left their church and were attending worship with Jeff and Kathy's congregation. People greeted them with open arms. A deputy sheriff said he'd see that patrols were more frequent around Marie's house. They caught a couple of high school students spray-painting the pink "F" on the front door. A Justice of the Peace fined them, with a great deal of reluctance, and ordered them to do forty hours of community service, including repainting the front of Marie's house.

And they waited and waited.

Then, a few weeks after Assembly, Pastor Esther came to Jeff's office. "Do you have a minute?" she asked. Her cheeks were flushed as she clutched a letter in a knotted fist.

"I'm going to be tried on charges," she exploded. "Me! By that rotten scum. He's filed charges against me with the Executive because I didn't contact him before sending the letter to the national body! Can you believe it?" She was pacing around the office, shaking the letter, and reading aloud the exact details of what was written. Finally, she calmed down enough to say, "This will be fun! You'd better believe that the investigating team's going to get an earful of what *he* did." She was steaming mad when she left Jeff's office. He knew there'd be some dust stirred up before this was over.

The day of Pastor Esther's trial arrived. Kathy, John, Marie, and Jeff were ready to testify as to what had taken place. A man strode into the room and up to the clerk of the meeting. He was wearing a tailored suit that looked like it must have cost at least a grand.

The meeting was gaveled into silence. Then the clerk asked, "Did you call Reverend Smith before you sent the above-mentioned letter to our national body?"

"No!" Pastor Esther responded. "But..."

She was interrupted by the clerk. I'm sure there must be more to your action. Why else would you have gone to the trouble you did? But it seems like the only relevant question is what you did ahead of time to work it out with the minister raising the charges You have been charged with a violation of your ordination vow 'to be a friend to your colleagues in ministry.' I believe that's all we can consider."

Jeff was stunned for a while before he stood and tried to get a word in, but it was too late.

"The judicial body will now recess to consider this matter."

That was all! Nobody could believe what had just happened. Barely five minutes had passed, no testimony, and the judicial body was making a decision. How could that be?

A half-hour later, the august body returned with a written statement. They looked at the well-tailored man who seemed to have swayed their deliberations, and nodded as if they'd followed his recommended action.

"Esther Samson, please stand," the clerk intoned. "You have been found to have broken your ordination vow to be a friend to your colleagues in ministry. We realize there are mitigating circumstances, but they are beyond the scope of what we were asked to consider. They are more relevant to any action you bring about him. You will be rebuked on the floor of our regional body at its next meeting. A member of this body has agreed to compose the rebuke, based on our deliberations. Is there a motion to adjourn?" And that was it.

They couldn't believe what had happened. Esther was going to be rebuked and nothing was going to be done to the man who'd brought on all the heartache, even though he had violated the sanctity of his pastoral counseling session with John.

As they milled about, one of the members of the judicial body cornered Esther to ask what had gone on to make her take such drastic action. The whole story tumbled out. Other members of the committee were drawn, out of curiosity, to the conversation. As the details of what happened to John were recounted, a look of astonishment covered many faces. "I wish I'd been privy to the whole story," one said. Several others affirmed their agreement. "Our decision might have been totally different if we'd known. But we were told, on good authority, that the details were unnecessary to our deliberation. We just assumed that was so and proceeded to take what seemed to be the only course, the mildest form of judgment we could make. We'll see what we can do to change it."

The day came for the regional body to meet. The action rebuking Pastor Esther was near the end of the agenda. Usually, by that time, few people were in attendance. After lunch, interminable reports were presented, one after another. The body was lulled into a kind of somnolent movement of motions made, seconded, explained perfunctorily and passed on a half-hearted "Aye." Sometimes with a trickle of "Nays" when the opportunity for opposition was given.

But this time was different. Mid-afternoon, when the report of the judicial body was to be presented, many people were still there. Others had returned to see if something *hot* was going to take place that would liven up this boring, but necessary, meeting.

The clerk of the judicial body walked up to the lectern to give the report. "Mr. Moderator, we have one action that needs to be handled that doesn't require a vote of the body. We have taken action to give a public rebuke to the Reverend Ms. Esther Samson."

"I move that the action be overturned," one delegate asserted. Hands flew up to be recognized.

"That motion is out of order," the clerk ruled. "The actions of the judicial body are not subject to the review of this body."

A flurry of other motions was offered, each trying to suggest a way to overturn the action of the judicial body. Even a member of the judicial body stood to speak in favor of an action. "I'd like this body to review the action," she said. "There was information concerning the allegation that we were not allowed to hear."

The judicial clerk responded, "That may be the case, but the details aren't relevant to this case, though they might be a part of charges brought against the plaintiff.

The body sat in silence. It was plain that Pastor Esther was going to be rebuked, no matter what happened. Then the stately older woman, who'd stood up on the floor of the national meeting to question the letter that had brought the rebuke, rose from her seat.

"I've come 700 miles to attend this meeting and I'm not going home without being heard," she said. Using all her regal stateliness, she purposefully walked up and stood right beside Esther. Ripples of movement began in the body, as people crawled around others to get out from their positions in the pews. Within a few minutes Esther was surrounded by people, many of whom she'd only known by name. And, of course, Jeff was there too—and Marie——and Kathy—and John, too. He'd been elected as a youth delegate to the meeting.

The group joined hands, circling Esther. As the clerk of the judicial body read the words of rebuke, the unspoken response from the spontaneous crowd proclaimed to all present that the rebuke encompassed all who stood with her.

And Jesus said, "Happy are you when people insult you and persecute you and tell all manner of evil things against you because you are my followers. Be happy and glad, for a great reward is kept for you in heaven. This is how the prophets who lived before you were persecuted."

Matthew 5:11–12 (TEV)

Written On The Heart

It was now an eyesore! It stood about head high and was all ragged and tangled. Almost like wheat shock that was buzz cut unevenly by a drunken barber. Once it had stood tall, a rich brown and vibrant tree—sometimes partially green and sometimes partially orange. But now it was an eyesore of heartwood remaining.

Every day on the way to work I had looked forward to seeing it. A beautiful piece of God's creation. I don't know what kind of tree it was. Somewhere back in my shortened Boy Scout/Cub Scout career I must have studied leaves and how to identify trees by their leaves. It had spread its limbs over a wide plot of ground, even hanging over the road. It provided a kind of live calendar for me. When its tender green leaves began to unfurl, I knew cold weather would lose its grip on my world soon. In summer when the leaves turn darker green, I'd eagerly await the colorful specter of fall. Because in fall the leaves turned a bright, vibrant orange. It had been a breathtaking orange I believed no dye could mimic. And as the orange slowly became a dirty blotched brown, the tree would present me with a waterfall of leaves. One crisp fall day I even stopped and stood under the tree and, whipped by the wind, let its gentle shower fall all over me. Even when it was denuded of leaves, the far-ranging limbs had a poetic grace as wind bent the, now, more brittle branches.

But it was now an eyesore. The heartwood all deformed and scraggly. Even after its demise I'd drive by, hoping against hope that it would reign there once again for me to enjoy. I'd watch the stump on the way back and forth from work, wondering when somebody would finally chop it down and pull it out by the roots that no longer could nourish. But nobody did. Week after week passed. Then it was month after month. The eyesore remained there, looking more like a bombed out relic of war than a majestic tree. When I happened to stop, I could see the searing burn slashes the bolt out of the blue had caused. I wish I could have been there at that tragedy to bid farewell to my friend, even though there would have been nothing I could have done to stop the carnage of the lightning storm.

Then one day, on my daily trek to work, I noticed a man hauling things out of the back of his truck. As I passed by I turned and saw him heft a chainsaw out of the pickup bed. I made a U-turn to see what he was going to do. Maybe it was to pay my final respects as the interment of a friend was taking place. But the man wasn't cutting the tree stump down. He was cutting around the stump, stopping every now and then to observe what he was doing. My attention riveted, I began to see a form take shape. I got out of my car to watch. Slowly the form began to turn into a big teddy bear. A teddy bear carrying a picnic basket of bread and honey. I'd glance down at my watch, hoping I could see the final outcome of the artist's handiwork before I had to go to work.

But that was not to be. Appointments beckoned, commitments called, work had to be attended to. So I left, looking back over my shoulder at intervals as I drove until I couldn't see anything but a brown blob. Even the whirring whine of the mechanical *brush* faded. I realized I needed to pay attention to my driving because I had drifted over into the on-coming lane. The blatt of a horn jerked me back to reality and I swerved back into my lane.

All day I wondered what the final work would look like. I'd be riding somewhere to visit a client, or reading a report, and the face of the bear would flit across my mind. The longer the day went along the more curious I got. What would it look like—this art made from the carnage of an old friend. My curiosity got the better of me, so I left work a full hour early. I took all the shortcuts I knew to get to the place where my friend the tree was being transformed into a work of art. When I finally got to that special place, the wooden statue, made out of a gross-looking old stump, was a sight to behold. The detail was astounding, each claw and eye and paw pad looked lifelike. Then I noticed that there was a new character in the sculpture—a little cub, prancing along beside the older bear, all excited about the adventure the two were on. Nestled in the grass at the front of the statue was a rustic wood sign with these words burned into it: *Teddy Bear's Picnic.*

The heartwood that had survived the crackling power of nature had been transformed from blight into beauty. Is this perhaps a parable of life?

> The Lord says, "The time is coming when I will make a new covenant with the people of Israel and with the people of Judah...I will put my law within them and write it on their hearts."
>
> Jeremiah 31: 31–33 (TEV)

Creating A Clean Heart

Steam still curled up from Pastor Don's first cup of coffee. Sermon writing time loomed. Friday had arrived and not a word was yet on paper. He convinced himself he needed to ease into the day by taking a gander at the newspaper. The bold headlines proclaimed *Saigon Falls*—something a rational part of the national mind knew might happen but the John Wayne part hoped would not. Don put aside the paper and his concerns and began to work on Psalm 51, the passage he'd chosen to preach from.

The scholarly study, the translation work, the word studies, and comparisons of similar passages had been done, but the finished project was nowhere in sight.

A faint tapping on the office door. Don ignored it. The tapping persisted. "Come in," he finally called. The light touch had made him think *child,* so he was surprised when the door tentatively opened and a man was standing there—a hulk of a man with slumped shoulders and downcast eyes. He almost filled the doorway. Don offered his hand, and the visitor swallowed it with both of his.

"I need to talk to...to a minister," he stammered. Don couldn't see how such a weak voice could come from such a huge man.

It was obvious he'd had physical fitness training. He looked like someone you'd want beside you if you had to venture down a dark alley at night. His buzz-cut shouted *military*, even though he wasn't in uniform. In addition to his formidable physical appearance, he had a commanding presence. Creases of concern etched his forehead and mouth—*officer*, Don assumed.

"I pass by this church every day on the way to work," the man mumbled. "I remember coming to Sunday school here as a kid. Can we talk?"

He hunkered down in the chair. Powerful hands gripped the arms so tightly his knuckles were white. A trip through a past that had weighted this powerful man down began.

"With Saigon falling and all, I just had to talk with somebody today. I used to go to Sunday school here—but I've already said that. I hoped there'd be someone to listen to me like my teacher used to when I was waiting for my folks to pick me up." He briefly looked up at me before reburying his gaze on his lap.

"I got back from Nam four years ago after doing two tours. I hadn't thought Saigon falling would get under my skin, but it has and there's a ton of stuff bustin' to come out."

"Go on," Pastor Don encouraged. The words were hardly out of his mouth before a tsunami of memories surged.

The veteran blasted the demonstrators who greeted his ship when he returned and poured blood on his freshly, pressed uniform. Then he reminisced about his Dad's return at the end of a war and compared it to the greeting he got in his hometown when he returned from "The Nam." For that there was a parade—for me nothing.

"When the bus stopped, only crazy Chester was there, waiting for the sheriff to put him in the pokey so he'd have a place to sleep. I asked Chester where everybody was and he told me, 'Dey's gone to the playoff game down ta the football field!' He looked at me as if I were the crazy one for not knowing."

Don's guest would occasionally look up before swiftly returning his gaze to his lap. He silently struggled with memories before more words poured out.

"I wasn't such a hero, in spite of all the medals I've shoved in the bottom drawer of the dresser. Like the time my three best sergeants were shootin' dope in Cholon."

He'd gathered a few guys to go get them. They locked them in the storeroom to *detox* because turning them over to the psych ward would probably get them in trouble with the Corps. He shook his head as he related that, after they'd been clean for a week, they disappeared again and were found dead with needles still sticking in their arms from the *hot shot* they'd gotten.

"I punched my hand through a wall when I found them," he groaned. Ever so slightly he began to sit more erect in the chair. "When I got out of the hospital, the company officers took me out for a night on the town. We hit many a joint and were pretty drunk by the time we got to a bar where the most beautiful Vietnamese woman was perched on a bar stool. She seemed to be waiting for someone. The guys starting hitting on her, but she ignored them and got up to leave. They started walking her out the door, making lewd comments and groping her. She turned to me with startled eyes looking like a deer caught in headlights. I rose from my chair, but sat back down and didn't do a single thing to help her. *Not-a-single-thing!*" He punctuated each word by slamming his hands on the chair arms. "I can still see her frightened eyes."

Don was so engrossed in the story he almost didn't notice the man was now erect enough to make direct eye contact. But he still slumped.

"We were short of lieutenants one day," he continued, "so I led a patrol with orders to seek out and destroy an enemy arms dump."

He admitted how scared they all were. Faulty maps made it hard for them to find the friendly village they had planned to use as a base of operations. Then they heard rapid firing. Thinking it was an attack, they headed for the *vill* nearby.

"When we got there," the man related, "we saw a man with a rifle in his hand, and a kid with a grenade. We opened fire and the bodies flew. The man with the rifle turned out to be carrying a shovel and the kid with the grenade—all he had was a round piece of fruit. A spent string of firecrackers lay near a freshly dug grave." He paused for a long time, then sobbed, "I...I shot the kid."

Don couldn't say a word. Seminary hadn't prepared him for such pain. The silence seemed to help the visitor. His tone softened as he went on.

"After that I don't remember a thing until I woke up on my cot two days later. Sometimes the scene will flash through my brain kinda like a flickering newsreel. I haven't had one of these flashbacks for a long time now, but I had one last night. When I saw the headline this morning something inside said it was time to get it all out. I didn't know if I'd be able to tell you, but now that I've started, I can't seem to stop."

Don noticed the man was sitting military straight in his chair now. He looked like the person one would have expected him to be—strong, confident, even his voice was firmer. Don moved his chair away from the desk in order to go to the man, but the veteran stood first.

"Thank you, Pastor, for listening," he said. He snapped to rigid attention, saluted, then executed a crisp about-face and walked out the door, closing it firmly behind him.

Don was thunderstruck as he tried to process

what had just happened, he looked down and Psalm 51 almost leapt off his desktop. It was then he could finally grasp the complete meaning of what the psalmist had written thousands of years before.

> Be merciful to me, O God, because of your constant love. Because of your great mercy, wipe away my sin...Create a pure heart in me, O God, and put a new and loyal spirit in me. Don't banish me from your presence...Give me again the joy that comes from your salvation...
>
> Psalm 51:1, 10, and 12 (TEV)

⌒

Two months later Don was settling into the morning with his coffee, the newspaper, and another sermon that needed writing. The headline, *Church World Service Honors Local Man,* jumped out at him.

The photo showed the man who had come into the church office. The tag line said: "...is being honored for outstanding work in resettling Vietnamese refugees. He was unable to accept the award in person because he was escorting forty orphans of the war..."

I Believe In God The Father

It's a seedy, run-down neighborhood. Boarded-up storefronts sit aside a few businesses hanging on through pure grit and determination. Most of the buildings are three stories high, with businesses on street level and residences on the other two. One can smell cooking grease from some of the eateries, gasoline emission pollutants from the disheveled cars that line the street, and a host of competing, undecipherable odors. Some autos look like they might run. Others have that sad, deserted look with little orange stickers plastered on them, indicating they are to be towed away for one reason or another. Poles with laundry drying on them stick out from some windows. It's a place urban redevelopment has forgotten.

One car would catch an observant person's eye. It's a wreck, just like all the others on the street. But this one has an occupant hunched down in the seat. Unless one would be looking for him, he'd be hard to spot. Clothed in the *haute couture* of poverty, his torn T-shirt can be seen through the window, along with a crumpled overcoat. The close observer would see the active eyes darting this way and that, looking at the left sideview mirror, right sideview mirror, followed by a glance into the rearview mirror. Then eyes back to the front. The man has a little gizmo he sometimes sticks up and peers through to see in all directions. But mostly his gaze is focused on a store that looks like it's boarded up. People seem to be going in and coming out frequently. Some are well dressed and stick out in the neighborhood. At times a fancy car drives up and its occupant exits the auto, looks around furtively and enters.

The man in the car is Jim Randall. He's a police officer—and a good one! For over twenty years he's enjoyed the plaudits of the people he has served, and also has suffered under their abuses. He is no brown-nosed sycophant, but yet he's been promoted several times. Presently, he's in charge of a squad of detectives who specialize in narcotics investigations. Those opposing Jim call him "The Narc." One could hardly guess from his stoic, protected exterior the empathetic nature of this man with a badge. He could have been a precinct chief, a homicide detective, a member of internal affairs—really anything he wanted to be in police work—but Jim chose narcotics. And there was a young man very special to him who played a significant role in the choice of that career.

∽

Early on—when Jim was a rookie—he and his partner had been called to investigate a tip. They'd gone to a run-down apartment/hotel. The front door was gaped open, belying the alarm system touted on a sign slapped whopper-jawed on it. As Jim walked up the stairs, his nostrils filled with an acrid combination of smells—disinfectant, antique urine, mold, and a United Nations of food odors. At the third floor landing he turned left down the corridor toward the apartment an informant had told them about. He could see his partner coming toward him from the other direction. They both were moving quietly, trying to make their approach as stealthily as they could. It had been reported that the woman in room 305 had shot a convenience store clerk during a robbery.

Jim's partner, Cal, was a seasoned police officer who had shunned promotions for his entire thirty-year career so he could *remain on the streets*. In tandem they arrived at the door. Cal knocked; the flimsy door seemed to be held to the jamb only by a thread of a hinge.

"Who is it?" a husky voice cried out.

"The police," Jim shouted. "Open up!"

There was a faint rustling inside the room—then a shot! The slug whizzed through the door and lodged in the peeling doorjamb across the hall. Jim put his foot to the door and kicked it open. Assuming the defensive stance he'd learned at the academy, he stepped into the room and saw a tousled woman drunkenly raise a gun for a second shot. Jim's gun barked first. The woman fell back on the bed, her head dangling over the side. Her upside-down eyes stared blankly at Jim. He knew she was dead. Jim felt her pulse only to confirm what the woman's eyes revealed. Cal nodded in agreement.

A muffled scream from the rumpled bedcovers caught their attention. Jim untangled the bed linen and discovered a naked baby. He guessed the boy to be only a few months old. This was a shock to both men as the snitch had told them nothing about a baby. Jim clutched the child to his chest, matching sob with sob.

Cal spoke into the radio on his shoulder: "Shots fired; suspect down; infant on site! Crime scene secured."

The infant looked up at Jim. His sobs quieted to soft snuffling sounds with an occasional hiccup. Then the exhausted young one snuggled securely into Jim's arms as though he'd known those arms for all of his short life.

Soon the room was filled with officers, a medical examiner, and paramedics who'd confirmed what Jim and his partner already knew. Child Protective Services (CPS) arrived, and Jim reluctantly turned the baby over to the social worker. Fellow officers comforted him in a gruff, warm-hearted way. The shooting team came and the whole investigation began in a whirl of questions and repeated answers. The activity helped to cover the horror of the fatal shooting, but nothing seemed to still the infant's wails that were etched on Jim's brain.

Back at the precinct house, he tried to type his report. He needed to focus, but all he could see were the eyes of the woman and their blank condemnation. He even caught himself typing "eyes" in the report and had to borrow WiteOut™ to erase the word. But the memory wasn't as easily blanked out.

When Jim got home, he told his wife about the baby. He made it sound like it would be a humane act to take in this motherless child, but Jennifer knew Jim needed this more than the baby did. So they wangled CPS into letting them be foster parents. They were able to get the necessary paperwork fast-tracked—no small feat when dealing with a protective bureaucracy. After several months and a frustrating barrage of examinations and interviews, they finally stood before a judge. James Randall Sr. was fairly bursting with pride when his adopted son, James Randall Jr., was placed into his arms. "Which Jim," became a family problem, so the young Jim soon became Deuce—for Jim the 2nd.

Six months later, Jim senior was working a crime scene when he got called back to the station. When he got there, the captain's face said it all. Jim heard his boss say "Randall" then an inner voice of disjointed phrases told him the rest of the story. Horrible accident—drunk driver—wife—couldn't avoid it—hit head on—dead.

Left side view mirror—right side view mirror—rearview mirror—front.

Scrunched down in the car, Jim remembers that night. A faint shudder ripples through his body. Lately he's been passing the long hours thinking back through Deuce's growing up years. The memories reach out to greet him and fill those hours on stake out.

Left sideview mirror—right sideview mirror—rearview mirror—front.

There'd been good times—like those when he held his son under the armpits while faltering little legs stumbled their first few steps forward. Or the day when the boy could walk on his own without being bolstered by his father.

Left sideview mirror—right sideview mirror—rearview mirror—front.

In the stillness of the car, Jim relishes the remembering times—like Deuce nestled in the crook of his arm while they read a story together. By the time he was four, Deuce could repeat the words of a story after it had been read to him only three or four times. But that made no difference to Deuce. "Read it again, Daddy," he'd say over and over again.

When he was four and a half, Deuce had even tried to impress some of Jim's friends. "I can read!" he told them. Then he picked up *'Twas the Night Before Christmas* and commenced "reading." Jim was the only one who noticed the book was upside down.

Left sideview mirror—right sideview mirror—rearview mirror—front.

Suddenly he thinks he sees the suspect. His heart

rate climbs and muscles tense as the man walks toward the car. It's not him. So Jim settles back down and recalls more.

There was the maiden lady next door. "The "unclaimed treasure" derisive neighbors had labeled her. Jim still can see her angry face and pursed lips as she rendered the verdict she'd give for the damage done to her window—again. That window had been broken over and over again by Deuce's errant fastballs. Ten broken windows in all. No matter what Jim said or did. No matter how much allowance Deuce had to spend on replacing the broken panes, there was only one place in the huge yard where the child would pitch. And if the tosses came in "high and inside" the spinster's window caught the ball.

A knot tenses Jim's stomach. He ignores it and repeats the action litany once more—left sideview mirror, right sideview mirror, rearview mirror, front.

But the knot remains.

There'd been a convenience store in the neighborhood. Deuce had started stealing candy there on the way home from middle school. Jim had made him pay double for the candy and insisted that he go down and apologize. But nothing kept Deuce from *lifting* the candy again, even when he had more than enough money in his pocket to pay for it. Jim despised those humiliating trips to the store to pay for what Deuce had stolen. He had trouble looking the storeowner in the eyes—he still did, even today.

Again—left sideview mirror, right sideview mirror, rearview mirror, front. But the angry owner's eyes are still there. That memory is no sooner past than a smell creeps into his memory.

Jim had smelled the sweet acrid odor he'd smelled so many times on the job wafting down from his son's bedroom. Deuce hadn't known his dad would be home early. Jim had been hoping to surprise his son with a pizza from a place on the other side of town. Deuce liked that pizza best and Jim had wanted to have a small birthday celebration for him. He'd found a silly card he thought the teenager would enjoy. And he'd stopped for *double chocolate chunk*—the kid's favorite ice cream. He opened the door and the celebration was over! And that was only the beginning.

Left sideview mirror—right sideview mirror—rearview mirror—front.

Tears crept into Jim's eyes as he remembered innocent infant eyes he'd seen from the beginning turning into a chemically crazed teenager's stare. The conglomerate of uppers and downers, pills and needles had once caused Deuce to stop breathing for agonizing seconds that had seemed like a lifetime. But Deuce had pulled out of it, been hospitalized, and had been clean for a day short of six months.

Sitting up a little to straighten his cramped back, Jim looked to the left sideview mirror—right sideview mirror—rearview mirror—front.

The beginnings of a smile crease the corners of his mouth. *He didn't miss a single day without going to a Narcotics Anonymous meeting. Sometimes he went two or three times a day.* The smile grows as Jim recalls Deuce chanting as he took each stair step down from his room to the main floor, "Come—back—it—works! Come—back—it—works! Come—back—it works!" Twelve steps—and a word for each step. Three times, three meetings. The creases of concern and worry begin to relax as the smile widens on his face.

Left sideview mirror—right sideview mirror—rearview mirror—front. And the stakeout ritual repeats itself again and again.

At midnight Jim decides to call it a day. He's been at it since early morning. *I guess the guy isn't coming.* He clicks on the radio and tells the dispatcher he's *heading for the barn.*

As he pulls his car into his driveway he remembers that Deuce is set to receive his Six-month Chip. "Six whole months!" Randall cries out loud in joy for the world to hear. "I think I'll fix something special for the anniversary. Corned beef and cabbage! It was one of Deuce's favorites when he was little.

Jim unlocks the side door and enters the kitchen. He scrounges around in the refrigerator, checks the pantry, then the freezer to see what he'll need to get at the store. A rumble in his stomach sends him back to the refrigerator where he moves things around to see what there is to eat. "Yuck," he mutters, when he finds a long-forgotten container with unidentifiable gray-green contents. *What's this,* he wonders, *breakfast? Dinner? Whatever!* He pushes more jars around then decides on cheese, crackers from the pantry, and dill pickles. He spreads this *gourmet* feast out on the kitchen table and grabs a chair. He throws newspapers on the floor to free the chair for sitting. He grins as he thinks about the big celebration they will be enjoying tomorrow.

When the phone rings, the cop habit kicks in and Jim glances at his watch to note the time of the call—1:33. "Randall here!" he speaks into a black rotary phone. He hasn't been able to install the new one he received as a Christmas gift—the one with speed dialing, answering machine, and all the other stuff he knew he'd never need, and probably couldn't figure out how to use anyway.

"Randall! This is Jackson downtown. I've got Deuce down here." In split seconds, Deuce's naked infant eyes, his toddler eyes, his defiant, errant pitcher eyes, and the recent "upper/downer" eyes all flash through Jim's mind.

"I don't know how to tell you this," the voice drones on, trying to hide any show of emotion, "but his feet are one pretty tracked-up mess. What do you want me to do with him? He's in a holding cell in case you want to *spring* him. No paperwork's started on him yet. What do you want me to do?"

"Hold him, Jack. I'll get back to you...and thanks, guy. I really appreciate this!" It takes several tries before Jim can get the phone on the cradle. He finally uses two hands to hold one still enough to respond to his brain's command.

"Oh, God!" he breathes through his teeth, "What do I do now?"

One voice inside his head says, *Let him rot in jail where he belongs. He's made his own bed, now let him lie in it!*

But, he's my son! The other side pleads. *I love him!*

The angry voice retorts: *But he's slapped me in the face by what he's done. I gave him food, a home, clothes, love, took him in when I didn't have to, gave him spending money—and he spends it on the junk I throw other people in jail for using!*

"But I gave him my name!—My name!" Randall screams at the top of his voice. "He's mine and no matter what he's done I still love him!"

Thoughts of a recent evening's work break through. *Two days ago I busted up a cocaine party and threw the book at a bunch of crazy college kids just about his age. Should I do this to my son?*

I've got to be consistent

But, Lord, how can I possibly do this to my own son?

These thoughts bounce back and forth in his mind like a fast-speed, ping pong game. When his heart won't let him keep up with the turmoil, he tries to block it all out by focusing on something else. He forces himself to look down at his watch and utters a painful snort—1:35. A mere two minutes have passed yet it seems like an eternity. The swirling muddle returns.

Should I go down to the station?

No, Let him get out of this one on his own!

But, he's my son...

The nerve—embarrassing me in front of Jackson and heaven knows who else. Will I have to quit the narc squad? Could his supplier be one of the dirtbags I've been trying to catch? What if I'd seen Deuce on my stakeout?"

Jim walks to the closet to get his coat. It's not there. He finally realizes he hasn't taken it off yet. He gropes for the keys in his pocket. They aren't there. He fumbles through all his pockets, pulls out a ballpoint pen and slams it to the floor in frustration. Then he remembers where he put the keys—on top of the refrigerator.

"He's my son!"

"Kick him out. You've done all you can for him! He's spitting in your face!"

As Jim reaches for the door, a quick breath like a sob sears through him and puts sound to the shapeless prayer, *Oh, God, I hurt!*

And, Officer James Randall walks out of the kitchen, out of the front door, locks it behind him, then treks down the steps to his waiting car—one—more—time.

The prophet Hosea tells us God's cry: *When Israel was a child, I loved him and called him out of Egypt as my son. But the more I called to him, the more he turned away from me. My people sacrificed to Baal…Yet I was the one who taught Israel to walk. I took my people up in my arms, but they didn't acknowledge that I took care of them. I drew them to me with heartstrings of love. I picked them up and held them to my cheek; I bent down to them and fed them.*

Ephraim! Ephraim! How can I give you up, Ephraim? . .My heart churns and my stomach turns into knots!

Ephraim! Ephraim! How can I give you up, Ephraim?
Selections from Hosea 11:1–8 (original translation)

Gone Fishin'

"Blast it!"

Lamar slams his palms on the handles of the lawn-mower. He angrily wipes a swath of dirt onto his forehead in an attempt to wipe away sweat. His clothes are grimy with grass clippings and dirt. It has turned from dusk to dark, and Lamar's upset because he has just re-mowed a portion of the church lawn he cut an hour ago. He bangs the off button, spins the mower around and heads for the shed at the back of the church property. On the way the mower lurches and Lamar sprawls over the handles. "Blast it!" he shouts. "When is somebody going to fill that hole in?"

"Where is everybody?" he complains vehemently. "I call a dadblasted workday and nobody shows up! Ken, Jack, and Jerry said they'd come, and Marie and Sophie!" Suddenly, Lamar realizes he's talking out loud and there's no one to hear him. *I always said a person had better worry when they start talking to them-selves,* he thinks sheepishly. *And you really need to worry when you start answering.* "Yep! That's true!" he says out loud before he can catch himself.

By the time he drifts off to sleep that night, Lamar's mood has changed from anger to frustration and disappointment over the lack of follow-through church folks have.

Lamar Klein is the kind of guy a church really needs. He's in charge of the Building and Grounds Committee and has taught the adult Sunday School class for years. And, if that isn't enough, he is also heading up the church pledge campaign for the third year in a row. In short, he's the kind of volunteer min-isters wish they could clone.

Sunday morning dawns bright and clear. Lamar is up and ready for church. A passing thought about the half-mowed churchyard flits across his mind. *The shaggy part's going to stick out like a sore thumb. I could have gotten up early this morning and done it,* he tells himself. A twinge of guilt hits him, followed by a sec-ond twinge—this one of anger.

When he gets to church, Lamar sees Ken and Jack. It's all he can do to greet them. Realizing he's being petty, he puts the Saturday workday behind him and decides *it'll be a great day!* Then he heads for the Sunday School class.

He has prepared a lesson he hopes will really get people involved. It's a juicy passage from the book of Amos, quite appropriate for the July Fourth festivities coming up soon. "Maybe even old Evan will say *something* today," John murmurs. "This lesson ought to be right down his alley."

By the time class is scheduled to start, only a handful have dribbled in, all of them sitting in the back row of folding chairs. Susie Drew hurries in on time but finds no empty seats in the back row, so she apologetically moves one from the middle row to the back and sits down.

There's a lethargic feel to the group. Lamar decides to have a cup of coffee, so he goes to the back of the classroom with his personal mug. The pot is empty! The switch on *Mr. Coffee*® is turned off. Closer inspection reveals stale coffee grounds. Lamar places his mug on the table and returns to the lectern to start the class.

He's just about to begin when another latecomer scurries in. The chair shuffling ritual is accomplished. Since all slots in the back, even makeshift ones, are occupied alternative ones on the sides are sought. No one wants to sit in the front.

Each time the lesson begins a new person tries to sneak in, usually with more fuss and furor than if they'd walked in boldly. But, in spite of the ragged start, Lamar is itching to get into the meat of what the prophet Amos had to say to folks of his day.

A good fifteen minutes into the class, the door creaks as Gerald tries to tiptoe in. Everyone watches as he unsuccessfully looks for a seat in the back row. Then the side of the room is hoped for—futilely.

Finally, he reluctantly plops down in the pariah section reserved for really latecomers—the front.

Lamar's stomach begins to growl and grumble. He remembers he didn't have that doughnut he was counting on. He'd purposely not eaten breakfast in anticipation of one of the few naughties he allowed himself—the Sunday morning doughnut. But, Gerald, the last one to arrive, bore no parcels. He'd forgotten the doughnuts he'd volunteered to bring.

The class bumbles along with Lamar carrying the load. No one offers an utterance of comment. All efforts to solicit participation are in vain. Lamar decides to try a discussion. He suggests the class break into small groups. Nobody moves. After an awkward silence, he suggests breaking into pairs. Again no response. Finally he numbers them off himself and prods them into spots around the room. The only eager participant in this activity is Gerald—he's relieved to be out of the odious center front position:

Lamar cajoles folks to talk. Finally one group, followed by another, then another begins to share. A surge of victory; it's false hope. One group of men is talking about a controversial baseball player trade. A second group—all women—is talking about the price of lettuce and wondering whether the alleged weather conditions really made the crop scarce, or if it was merely an excuse to boost prices. The third group—mixed men and women—were talking about three things at once, none of which remotely approaches the suggested topic.

Lamar's frustration level is maxed out, so he scrappes the lesson for the day, deciding to save it for next week. He really needs to get to the Finance Office early, so he leaves the class to fellowship. Today is the deadline—in fact, the extended deadline—to turn in the pledge campaign reports.

Frank sticks his head in the office door. "I know today was the deadline for the group-visit reports," he offers, "but my group is lagging behind." As he leaves, he looks over his shoulder and adds, "I'll get it to you next Sunday, or the next—or..." His voice trails off as he walks away.

Eunice ventures in. "My campaign booklet got lost, and I haven't had time to trace it down. Mother! is in town with her white glove on, checking my whole house for dust or other signs of slovenly housekeeping."

As she complains, Lamar watches other group leaders walk by the door on their way to worship. No one even bothers to stick his or her head in to report. They—just—walk—by. Finally Lamar hails Geoff and stops him in the hall. "You got your campaign report?"

"Was this the day they were due? I'll check into it this week. Next week for sure!"

Defeated in his efforts, Lamar leaves the Finance Office and heads into worship. He has a hard time getting his mind focused on the liturgy. Once he remains seated when everyone else has risen to sing. On the way to standing, he fumbles for his bulletin to find the hymn number. The bulletin falls to the floor. When he reaches down to retrieve it, the hymnbook falls out of his hand. Fortunately the noise is covered by the swelling chords of the organ. From then on Lamar stands, sits, and bows his head at the appropriate times, but is really on automatic pilot. He doesn't even know when the sermon is over until the moment of silence at the end jars him back to worship. He's been running through his mind the people he'll need to contact this week to help with the yard work this coming Saturday.

The Pastoral Prayer allows Lamar's mind an opportunity to wander again. He makes a mental checklist of who needs to be contacted for the pledge drive and when the best time is to reach them. He's barely halfway through his plan when he realizes he won't be able to get to the city to see the auto show. He's been looking forward to it as his car is on its last gasp. He always goes to auto shows so he can sit in the cars and check them out and get an idea of prices before a salesperson is breathing down his neck trying to *close* him.

His thoughts get into a muddle so he slams his hymnbook shut during one of those quiet times that descend on a worship service. He looks around rather sheepishly, then faces front to try to refocus on what is going on. Finally the Benediction is given and the organ swells into the Postlude—worship is over.

On the way out, Lamar buttonholes a few Building and Grounds folks and Pledge Drive volunteers.

Each one gives a vague, evasive answer. So he gives up and goes home.

At home his favorite chair beckons after he prepares a slap-dash lunch. He kicks back with a sandwich in one hand and an ice-cold soda in the other. He settles in to watch a baseball game, but keeps losing track of the action because he's distracted by church concerns. He gives up on the game and decides to make some inroads in the computer project he's brought home from work. That endeavor fares worse than the game. His mind keeps running over the pledge drive stuff, and the yard work. Work on the project is futile, so he tries television again. He "channel-surfs" and finds a shoot-'em-up western. He thinks this will do the trick. Black hats and white hats—he should be able to keep that simplistic plot straight. But church concerns keep drawing him away. He misses the crux of the conflict and can't reconstruct it, so the channel changer gets another workout. He settles on a spy movie involving a plot to assassinate the president. Finally diversion is attained.

The next Sunday, as people arrive for Sunday school, it's as clear as the nose on your face that the churchyard looks awful. Flowerbeds are partially weeded. The lawn is scraggly, two different heights of scraggly. And the persistent weeds have sprouted even more, some of them knee high. If one looks closely, there is one portion in which a deeper scraggly patch begins abruptly in a swath just about wide enough for a mower to have stopped in mid swipe.

The minister is the first to notice. He makes a mental note to check on this. He's in his study getting things ready for the worship service when there's an anxious knock on the door. "Pastor," a worried member queries. "Pastor, there's nobody to teach the adult class. They're all there and nobody knows where Lamar Klein is, or who's supposed to sub for him."

The minister drops his preparations and heads for the class, trying to figure out an emergency lesson plan to use. About the time he gets to the door, all he can come up with is a study he had been doing for next week's sermon. *Hope nobody remembers when next week rolls around,* he thinks anxiously.

There's no coffee and no doughnuts in the adult classroom, but the class time is filled. That's about all you can say for it. The minister dashes back to get ready for worship. He's just into his sermon review again when someone else knocks. "Pastor, who do we give the pledge campaign reports to?" He notices several people standing outside the Finance Office. "It's locked," one of them offers. "Do you know where Lamar Klein is? He's supposed to be here to receive our pledge campaign reports."

The minister unlocks the door and puts the stack of reports on the desk. "One of you, please stay in case others have results to turn in." They look from one to the other. They are in the midst of this hesitation waltz when the minister leaves, rather frantic by now.

He's had no time to get organized for worship. And here it is, already time to pray with the choir. In the midst of the last minute frenzy he makes a mental note: he must check in on Lamar—right after the service is over.

Worship ends and the last stragglers are folding into their cars. The minister remembers his mental note to check in on the missing Lamar. He sheds himself of his worship garb and heads for his car. He notices the dry grass clippings blowing around in the lightly swirling wind. It's obvious they've been around for some time. As he drives out of the lot, he wonders whether the Building and Grounds Committee has purchased a bagger or a mulcher attachment. He has no idea—Lamar always takes care of things like that.

When he gets to Lamar's house, he walks up the steps and knocks on the door. No response. He knocks again. Not a sound. He raps a third time. Again no answer. He walks around to see if anyone is in the backyard. No sign of yardwork going on—and no Lamar.

He peeks into the garage through a little window. No car. No Lamar? No car? Then the pastor remembers a small piece of paper fluttering on the mailbox by the front door. He rushes over and grabs the piece of paper. He looks at it. And looks at it again. A puzzled frown creases his face. Written on the sheet is *John* 21:3!

The minister makes a beeline for his car where he's left his Bible. He flips to the gospel of John. He thumbs through the picture of Jesus, the long section when the Lord's supper was begun, the death of Jesus, then to when the apostles had been scared to death that the authorities would come get them. They were behind closed doors, defeated and afraid. They thought the marvelous journey with their Master had ended in failure. And then the pastor finds the verse:

Simon Peter said to the others, "I'm going fishing."
John 21:3 (original paraphrase from the Greek)

Phoenix Syndrome: Hope Among The Ashes

The Ellis family sat up all night watching weather reports and listening to the radio. Things looked bad. Radar pictures showed whirling circles of clouds moving in over the small peninsula where they'd spent so many happy times as a family. They watched the storm of the century move closer and closer until the well-defined center moved onto land just to the west of that place of magic memories.

The whole area had been evacuated, so they couldn't get direct reports. But Jeff's imagination was doing a vivid job of picturing the destructive twelve to fifteen foot storm surges the weathermen talked about. He could almost see the waves swirling around their beach house.

Details of the summer home were sharp in his

mind. He hoped against hope it would still be standing, despite the fact that the whole peninsula at its highest point was only eight feet above sea level.

Jeff must have slept some during the night because he remembers dreaming of the house standing in the churning cauldron of water—standing tall, even though the water was up to the sun porch on the second story. He watched the water roiling around the bottom area where the cars would have been parked. He was even able to see the pilings holding firm against the worst hurricane that had struck that area in recorded memory.

In the morning, the weatherman announced the eye of the storm had moved inland, skirting the highway the family traveled on to go to the beach. They relaxed a bit. But then their worries came closer to home as they watched the deadly weather mass heading right for them. Even though they lived seventy-five miles inland, local warnings were issued to batten down for some damage. When the winds hit, they were fierce. They howled over the house and seeped through cracks the family hadn't realized were there. The back screen door kept blowing loose, banging back and forth until someone could go to relatch it. Every member of the family got soaked at least once while re-fastening the errant screen.

The next morning pine limbs were everywhere and cones lay all over the ground like brown snow. The mailbox had blown down, and a few shingles were missing. It was only then that Jeff was ready to admit his vision of the previous night—the one about the beach house riding out the storm—must have been a dream. How could the house possibly be standing when it had been through far worse than the family had inland?

Jeff joined the whole family trying to clean up the mess in their yard. He was picking up a few of the smaller branches, when, almost simultaneously, everyone blurted out, "I want to know! How's the beach house?"

It was a special place. Mr. Ellis' work had uprooted them from Texas three times, California twice, Oklahoma, Virginia and North Carolina once. And they had even spent time in Germany and Japan. Though they only used the beach house a month or more each summer, it was the place in Jeff's childhood where his roots grew deeper than anyplace else. It was *home*.

For the next few days the radio blared while they cleaned up. Each night was spent glued to the TV watching news reports to find out when the all-clear would be given so they could go where they all wanted to be. The days moved in honey slowness until it was safe to leave. All they had to do was jump in the car! Everything had been packed up and loaded several days before.

They drove down the highway pointing out the damage as they went. At first they noted only a few trees knocked down and the evidence of debris having been cleaned away. Then they saw familiar billboards blown over in heaps. Further along *changed* became *dis-*

appeared. Jeff had his mouth set for an ice cream cone at the special place that made *the best Dairy Queen™ cones ever.* When they reached it, a *Closed* sign greeted them—though the sign was superfluous since blown out windows and other wreckage told the story.

The gas tank needed filling, but Mr. Ellis didn't even think about stopping at one of the stations he passed. He always stopped at Mr. Watson's Texaco. When Jeff was a kid, Mom and Dad didn't know it, but Mr. Watson always gave him candy when they weren't looking. The low-fuel warning light on the dashboard came on before Mr. Ellis finally realized he had driven past the station. They had to drive back for gas.

He backtracked, but drove past the site twice before they saw the whirl of metal that had been the awning of Mr. Watson's station. It was spread out on the wrong side of the highway. Gassed up, they turned around and traveled toward the unknown. The further they went, the fewer the buildings. Even utility poles were dominoed flat all along the road.

By the time the Ellis family neared the beach there was little they could recognize. They had to hunt around to find the road they should turn down. The houses were a shambles of pillars, pilings and strewn debris. Finally, Mr. Ellis found where their street had been when, by pure chance, he had noticed the weathervane that had been atop their house. It was buried upside-down in sand by the edge of the highway. From that point on, the spider web of streets and trails was impassable. So the family left their car and started to walk, looking carefully where they stepped.

Further and further they trekked, reaching the now-gentle water. They still hadn't seen the house, nor were they certain where it had been. Even though they knew it must be gone, they still hoped against hope that it might still be standing. A huge swimming pool, two houses down, finally gave them their bearings. From there they could see where the pilings of the seawall had been. Mr. Ellis chuckled when he remembered the meeting during which the contractor had sold him on *the final solution to making this home safe from whatever would come from the sea.* The once-formidable pilings were tossed about like a bunch of toothpicks on a canapé tray. It was only then that they could locate the septic tank; the flush-to-the-ground concrete monolith was all that was left of their beach home. They kicked around in the wreckage, but nothing recognizable remained.

The only thing left standing in the whole area was the swimming pool two houses down. It stood like a huge bathtub, the ground washed away from its sides until it looked a lot like a strange piece of wreckage that had been washed ashore or had fallen from the sky.

Jeff was the only member of the family who went to explore the beached whale of a pool. As he picked his way toward it, he noticed patches of green poking through the sand. Tiny plants were already regaining their foothold. He bent over to look at them up close and heard a strange, snuffling sound. Looking around, he found nothing. So he followed the sound and continued the hunt. Soon he was up to the land side of the undermined swimming pool. The sound seemed to be coming from a protected lip of the pool. As Jeff approached, the snuffling turned into a low, warning growl. It was then that he saw a mother hound lying on her side nursing six, brand-spanking new puppies. The sand was a little blood-stained in places. The dog must have sensed Jeff meant her no harm because she stopped growling and resumed snuffling. Lovingly she was licking each newborn until its coat glistened.

I am the Lord, who opens a way through the waters, making a path right through the sea. I called for the mighty army of Egypt with all its chariots and horses, to lie beneath the waves, dead, their lives snuffed out like candlewicks.

But forget all that—it is nothing compared to what I'm going to do! For I'm going to do a brand new thing. See, I have already begun! Don't you see it? I will make a road through the wilderness of the world for my people to go home, and create rivers for them in the desert! The wild animals in the fields will thank me, the jackals and ostriches too, for giving them water in the wilderness; yes, springs in the desert, so that my people, my chosen ones, can be refreshed. I have made Israel for myself, and these my people will some day honor me before the world.

Isaiah 43:15–21 (paraphrase from
the original Hebrew)

Pro Bono Publico

It's a hot dusty road, a snake-like thing winding among gulches and arroyos in a vast wilderness. Plants dwarfed by drought and heat struggle for life. The few animals that might inhabit this desolation have long since had the sense to burrow in someplace to escape the ferocity of the elements. But a human, a man on horseback, lacks the sense other critters have. His eyes blearily stare about the bleakness randomly, vacantly, as though the only thing observed is in his mind. He sits tall in the saddle or, at least, would sit tall if he weren't sagging from side to side, reacting automatically to the gait of the horse.

The horse stops and the man wakens from his fantasy about a cool spring of water and sees an obstruction of man, not nature. Briefly, his thoughts wander back to the reverie, but another liquid grabs his attention. He dreams of a sip of that amber liquid which—

as occasion and circumstance demand—can either warm the freezing or cool the burning. Of course, the longing is the same even in the opposites.

The man sits bolt upright in the saddle when he notices a thin ribbon of green winding its way down the random arroyo he's been following. Wiping his eyes to make sure it's not a mirage, he sees rows of short squat stones rowed up neatly one after the other on either side of the road. Finally, he works it out. It's a long, stretched out graveyard. Curiosity lures him to continue on the trail in hopes that the stretch of green might harbor liquid to refresh his parched mouth. He spies a hand pump with a spigot pointing toward a narrow, shallow trench that moves along each line of markers. His brain registers that the spigot might hold water. But his hopes are dashed when he spies a large lock, looped through the handle and attached to the pump.

After a prodigious bend in the road (one that would bring joy to the heart of a Southern highway planner) he notices a widening of the gulch. Then there's another twist—a more gradual one—that opens up into a narrow valley. Nestled in the farthest end is a small community. The community has a sense of order to it. All the streets look like they've been laid out by some divine protractor. Houses and other buildings are lined up precisely on either side of the perpendicular streets.

Splitting the town's neat symmetry is one street a little wider than the rest. At its far end is the largest structure in the community, a church with a glistening white spire reaching to the heavens. In fact, the entire town is bright white—as though there'd been some huge-scale sale on white semi-gloss paint. Beyond the church is a continuing of the parched plain which gradually narrows again into another gulch. The glaring whiteness seems rather like a lighthouse, warning evil not to come near.

The man on horseback, using his arm to blunt the glare, looks from side to side as he rides down the main street, hoping to see the much desired *Saloon* sign. Overhead, a fluttering banner stretches across the street and is secured on either side with a neat bow. In florid script adorned with daisies and roses, the banner says:

WELCOME TO ANGEL GULCH
from the
A.G.O.S.S.I.P. CLUB

The man continues slowly through town still on his amber liquid quest. The buildings are uniformly spaced and dazzling to the eye, except for one blackened gap. Instinctively, the man rides toward it. He stops his horse in front of the dilapidated structure. Closer inspection reveals a weather-beaten sign—*The Seat of Sodom Saloon.* The rider's throat begins to quiver in anticipation of the cooling amber trickle that will soon wend its way down to his stomach, purging the parched feeling in his throat as it travels through.

Swinging doors hang loosely on their hinges,

swaying gently with the wind. The man thinks they look like a pair of hands inviting him in. As he touches one of them, it falls off its hinges with a heaven-shaking crash. Inside, cobwebs have conquered; dust is supreme. Crestfallen, the man looks from side to side. His spirits plummet. The shelves behind the bar contain a chorus of bottles, lined up neatly with their labels soaked off. They're all empty. Piles of glasses are symmetrically arranged in a stencil-weave down the center of the bar. Muttering a colorful oath under his breath, he turns to leave. Then he sees her.

A woman is framed in the entrance of the saloon. As she approaches he notices she looks like the archetypal mother. Her hair is piled up neatly on the top of her head, only a few wisps escaping the combs holding it in place. She's wearing a sensible housedress—nice enough for around the house, but not dressy enough for going out.

"A-hem," she clears her throat to be noticed. "Excuse me, Mister-ah-"

"Backus, ma'am, Jack Backus."

"I'm Mrs. Smith. I wasn't expecting to find anyone here, Mr. Backus. Excuse my appearance, but I was coming here to clean up with some of my club members. You must have seen our banner as you came into town. You can't miss it. We're the *Angel Gulch Order for Serving Society in a Petticoat.* Or as townsfolk here shorten it, the A.G.O.S.S.I.P. CLUB." She purred with the faintest hint of Deep South in her voice. "Oh, I'm forgetting my manners. Can I offer you a glass of lemonade? It's fresh squeezed just this morning."

"I'd prefer something a mite stronger," Backus answers.

"I'll bet you would—being on that dusty road for so long—but lemonade's all I can offer. My husband has the town bottle." She says this with obvious pride.

"The town bottle?"

"Yes, the town bottle—the only one in town we can get to without either Prudence's key or the one that Mrs. Tankton Sherman keeps on a chain dangling in her bosom."

Resignedly, Backus accepts the proffered beverage. He lifts it to his lips and drinks it in greedy gulps. "Might I have some more? It tastes mighty good. Well not as good as a whisky, but mighty good anyway."

She pours a refill and he drains it at a more sedate pace, with generous swipes of his mouth with a dust-encrusted sleeve.

A second woman enters. She's tall and angular, dressed in gray from chin to shin. .

"Prudence, how nice to see you. Do you see any of the others? We've got a lot to do to get this place set up for my husband." The two ladies busy themselves dusting and straightening. Prudence seems particularly interested in polishing the wooden door at the back of the main room. Occasionally she looks around to see if anyone is watching and surreptitiously gives the knob a tentative twist. It's locked.

More women enter the Seat of Sodom Saloon and

get quickly to work. Each is introduced to Backus and curtsies demurely. Backus acknowledges each by doffing his hat. However, action comes to a complete halt when they hear the creaking and groaning of the wooden sidewalk. The remaining swinging door crashes down, propelled by the hand of the last woman to enter.

She's 60-something. It seems like the room gets darker because she fills the entire doorway. Her dress is a severe black bombazine, with black buttons tightly spaced from the waist to the throat. Hints of gray make a telltale testimony of the true color of her hair, which mostly is an iridescent, unnatural, raven black. She strides into the room and imperiously surveys the work underway. She nods with approval at some, then centers in on Prudence. With a beady stare she glares at her still polishing the door. Unaware of her habit, she fingers a lump hidden between her headlight-like breasts.

"Oh, where are my manners?" Mrs. Smith says flustered. "Mr. Backus, may I present Mrs. Tankton Sherman, the president of our club." Nervously twisting the rag in her hands, she looks back and forth at Mrs. Sherman and Backus. The newcomer in black doesn't respond. To cover the silence, Mrs. Smith asks, "Can I offer you some more lemonade, Mr. Backus?" She begins to pour when a thunderclap of a voice interrupts her.

"Mrs. Smith," blasts Mrs. Sherman, "Have all your English teaching skills departed from your mind? It's

May I not *Can I!* Do you want this—er—man to think we're illiterate rubes?"

Startled, Mrs. Smith pours lemonade on Backus' boot. She stoops to wipe up the offending spill when another bellow comes. "For heaven's sake, forget his boot, tend to the floor. We have to get things ready for your husband who is making such a sacrifice for our children." Mrs. Smith quickly redirects her wiping.

"Backus, would you be so good as to arrange some chairs for us," Mrs. Sherman says with no thought of his not complying with her request.

Backus busily attends to his chore. When the president decides the room is well-prepared, she commands, "Sit!" All in the room select a chair, including Backus. "Not you!" Sherman pronounces, leveling a stern finger in his direction. "You are *not* a member of our club and have no business pretending to be one. You don't qualify on several accounts, the least of which is being a male." Before he can move from his chair, she turns her attention to the gathered ladies.

"A reading of the minutes of the Angel Gulch Order of Serving Society in a Petticoat, Prudence?"

Prudence begins to read in a monotone voice. Then there's a crash, and a man reeking of liquor stumbles into the gathered assembly. He throws an empty bottle (label removed) on the floor and shatters it.

"I just can't do it!" he screams. "It's too much to ask of me! This vile stuff tastes like horse tonic and upsets my stomach. I've sprinkled some of it on me and staggered around town just for show, but I just can't do this any more!"

"You've lost your resolve, Mr. Smith?" Mrs. Sherman asks. "You've forgotten the solemn oath you took only a day ago? Only one day ago! What's going to become of our children now that you've shirked your duty? They will all be led to perdition because of you. How can our children know about sin and evil without you? When they go out into the world, they'll be lambs led to the slaughter of sin because they won't know how to deal with temptation. In our fine town we've conquered sin and our children will be easy prey to evil when they leave here because we haven't prepared them to valiantly fight the meanness out there in the world. They won't have experienced evil and won't know how to fend it off."

Mrs. Sherman stops for a breath and realizes that nobody is listening. The failure of a man has fallen to the floor, banging it with his head and fists. He mutters and groans over and over, castigating himself for his inability to perform, punctuated by fits of furious crying.

The chattering of the women rises and falls. Everyone is wondering what to do. Conversation jumps from one topic to another, interspersed with possibilities for action. Backus gives up trying to keep track of the flow of conversation. He stares at the bar, alternately looking at the empty bottles and the glasses artistically arranged on the counter. Then their attention is refocused by several powerful pounding stamps of Mrs. Sherman's foot.

"Will the meeting come to order?" Miss Prudence is still whispering. More stamping. "Will the meeting come to order!" Prudence continues to whisper, pointing to Backus. More stamping. "Shut up, Prudence!" Mrs. Sherman shouts. Prudence flushes a bright pink and commences to fiddle with pen and pencil.

"We'll wave the reading of the minutes." Sherman is interrupted by a wail from Mr. Smith. "Control your husband, Mrs. Smith! Pray have him regain possession of his senses. Our first item of business is what shall we do now so that our children can experience sin and thus know how to handle it. Dr. Smith isn't going to be the town drunk so we've got to find another solution."

"Oh!" shrieks Miss Prudence.

"Do you have something to suggest, Prudence?" Mrs. Sherman queries.

Blushing again, Prudence stammers, "No! I stuck myself with my pencil."

Obviously restraining herself, Mrs. Sherman continues, "Any other ideas?" A few are offered and shot down by the moderator. Then Prudence squeaks. Eyes once again focus on her.

"What do you have to contribute, Prudence?"

"Nothing. I stuck myself again with this silly pencil," she stammers, lifting up the offending pencil for all to see.

With an even sterner glare at the gray-clad spinster, Mrs. Sherman continues.

Seconds later, Prudence clears her throat to be noticed. Mrs. Sherman ignores the interruption and continues to try to extract some further possibilities. Prudence again clears her throat.

"Shut up! Prudence!"

With a tentative wave of her handkerchief, Prudence again clears her throat to be recognized.

"Shut up, Prudence! Kindly put your pencil in a place where you won't be sticking yourself anymore. While we're trying to come up with solutions, I believe we need to thank Mr. Smith for trying, even though he has failed abysmally."

Prudence ventures more than just throat clearing, "I have..."

She's interrupted. "Shut up, Prudence! How many times must I tell you. Where was I—oh, yes—I commend Mr. Smith for his unselfish community spirit in aiding the morals of our children."

"Ah," again from Prudence.

"What is it?" Mrs. Sherman says menacingly. "You're interrupting our meeting, again. Do you have something to add? Something helpful? Are you capable of making a viable suggestion?"

Prudence, embarrassed almost to the point of incoherence stammers, "Maybe we have someone here who could help."

"Who could that possibly be? We've asked everyone in town to be the honored town drunk. And nobody accepted, except for Mr. Smith here..." Mr. Smith's wails make her raise her voice almost to a shout. "Except for Mr. Smith here, after I brow-be..., prevailed upon him to perform the service."

At this, Backus perks up.

"Well," Prudence timidly offers, "maybe there is someone. Maybe Mr. Backus, who just came into town, might be a candidate. I've noticed him looking longingly at the empty bottles behind the bar. He's even licked his lips as he's been looking."

"Yes, he *did* ask me for a drink of whisky and seemed mighty disappointed that our saloon didn't have any," Mrs. Smith recalls. " What about it Mr. Backus?"

"It's not up to you to offer anything, Mrs. Smith— you, whose husband wasn't willing to sacrifice for our children." Mrs. Sherman punctuates each word with stabs of her finger. Finally, she seems to realize the good sense the suggestion makes, so she asks, "What about it, Mister—er—Baker?"

"It's Backus, ma'am, Backus."

Backus draws himself up to his full height, takes his hat off his head and purposefully places it over his heart. "I just might be talked into it, ma'am—for the right price and a guarantee of good whiskey always near me, I just might be talked into it."

The ladies start to buzz excitedly. Even Mr. Smith stops crying and edges up on one elbow to see if it could possibly be true that he is to be relieved of his responsibility. The room is in an uproar until called to order by repeated stomping of Mrs. Sherman's powerful foot.

"Order, ladies, Order—Order, ladies—and-er-gentlemen." Slowly the conversation ceases. "Our next item of business is to check out the liquor supply. I believe we had stockpiled 30 cases of whiskey…"

Mrs. Smith interrupts, "That should be 40 cases, I believe."

"No, 30—I distinctly remember authorizing the purchase and shipping of 30." She shuffles among her papers for the invoice. "Yes, it says right here—30."

In actuality, the paper truly does show 40. Mrs. Sherman wads up the invoice in dispute and pushes it down the front of her bosom where no one would dare pursue it. Covering her need to be rid of the paper, she forcefully says, "I'll fetch my key and we'll see what's there." With ceremony she slowly pulls up a silver chain. Attached to the bottom is a key.

"Prudence, you're carrying your key, aren't you?"

"I thought there were only 20 cases of whisky ordered," Prudence counters. "I'm sure I remember right." She looks furtively from side to side. "Maybe that invoice was wrong and they delivered only 20."

"Shut up, Prudence, and pull up your key."

Flustered, Prudence slowly complies and, after some suspense, her key is deftly extricated from its protected position in her bosom.

By now Backus' attention is riveted on the door at the back of the room where he has surmised the liquor is stored.

Mr. Smith has rallied and offers to unlock the storeroom. He makes a display of placing the key in the lock and slowly turns it. The door opens. Smith stammers, "There's not any 40 cases here, not even 30—maybe 15 or 20, but no more." Eyes center in on Mrs. Sherman, then Prudence.

"You two are the only ones who could get into this storeroom. Explain."

Each does her best to look innocent, but neither succeeds. Backus gets them both off the hook by running into the room. He cracks open one case and extracts a labeled bottle. Lifting it up to the light, he looks lovingly at the amber liquid gently sloshing from side to side. With a smack of his lips in anticipation, he uncorks the bottle and takes a long draught of the liquor. He wipes his mouth with a grimy sleeve, then takes another even longer draught. By the time the bottle is half-empty the folks begin to look around again for Prudence and Mrs. Sherman. Each has a sufficiently sheepish look on her face.

Mr. Smith breaks the silence, "It's time we installed Mr. Backus here in the important, official office of *town drunk*."

He leads the people out to the glistening sidewalk. By now a crowd has gathered, wondering what the commotion is all about.

Solemnly Mr. Smith asks Backus, "Repeat after me! On my honor—"

"On my honor—"

"I will do my best—"

"I will do my best—"

"To do my duty—"

"To do my duty—"

"To Angel Gulch and its children—"

"To Angel Gulch and its children—"

"to stay as drunk as I can—"

"To stay as drunk as I can—" responds Backus with grateful seriousness, reminiscent of Br'er Rabbit and the Briarpatch.

While the crowd's attention is diverted by Backus' swearing in ceremony, Mrs. Tankton Sherman and Prudence Page slip back into the saloon storeroom. Each one surreptitiously takes a bottle from the opened case and takes a long drink—then another—and another. When they realize the ceremony is about over, each one straightens her skirt, waves a handkerchief in front of her mouth and quickly walks to the back of the crowd—hoping no one has noticed her absence.

> And Jesus said, "How terrible for you, teachers of the Law and Pharisees! You hypocrites! You clean the outside of your cup and plate, while the inside is full of what you have gotten by violence and selfishness. Blind Pharisee! Clean what is inside the cup first, and then the outside will be clean too...on the outside you appear good to everybody, but inside you are full of hypocrisy and sin."
>
> Matthew 23:25-6 (TEV)

Seeking Mona Smith

She was scared as she got off the plane. "Gerald," she said almost out loud. "Gerald, put your hand at the small of my back." And though there was no Gerald beside her—and there hadn't been for five years now—you could see her shoulders square some as she walked more purposefully toward the terminal. *Bienvenidos a Cancun*—the sign read.

Mona was flanked by two women, two friends. Though she still was apprehensive, even with the imaginary hand at the small of her back, she tried to look excited and ready for fun because that's what her friends were feeling. *Anxiety will just have to do for excitement*," she told herself.

Like a reverse funnel, the stream of people leaving the airplane entered Cancun airport and spread out to the tables where their luggage and papers were to be checked. The table where Mona ended up was presided over by a short, smiling young man who could hardly have been over five feet, four inches tall. Unobtrusively, she slipped out of her high heels and stood in her stocking feet, three inches shorter, while he checked her papers. *I wouldn't want to embarrass him, he seems so nice,* she decided. She wasn't sure, but she thought he somehow seemed surer of himself and more manly when she was closer to his height than when she walked up—so tall. Her mother had told her over and over, "The man *must* always be taller—or, at least, feel that he's taller. You do what you have to do to see to it." Mona caught herself just before she said, "Yes, Mother" out loud. She wondered why the old insecurities were stronger today—maybe it was the new place.

Mona put her *happy trip* face back on again when they got out of the airport terminal. She even felt bold enough to step off the curb and put two fingers in her mouth and whistle for a cab. "I haven't done that in years," she told her friends.

A cab zoomed up and the three of them—baggage and all—piled in. The drive into Cancun was exotic. The squat dense foliage seemed almost like a menacing dark green wall. Mona fantasized about what strange creatures must be living out there. She felt a trickle of sweat ooze down her chest. Her blouse matted to her back and the hair on her forehead and nape of her neck began to get damp. *I always wondered what happened to the Mayan culture,* she joked to herself. *Why it disappeared. Now I know! They didn't have*

a religious revolution or a plague or a popular rebellion.
They sweated to death—down to a puddle, she chuckled,
as she pictured how that theory title would look in
Anthropology in Review: "Perspiration brings end to
Mayan culture."

As they were whisked into the hotel porte-cochere,
the driver helped with the baggage, putting it inside
the door by the registration desk.

"You watch the luggage, Mona," one friend said,
"And we'll go check in."

The desk clerk kept riffling through the registration files. Her friends were getting more flustered by
the minute. Finally one came over to Mona. "They
can't find any reservation for Mona Smith." So her
friend gave some money to a porter to take care of the
luggage and Mona and her friend went to the desk to
sort things out.

"Reservations for Mrs. Gerald Smith, *por favor,*"
Mona said and, like magic, the reservation appeared
under *Gerald Smith.*

"I never would have worked that out, Mona. Can't
you let him go?"

Her friend's comment stung her. She knew nothing hurtful was intended, but it stung just the same.
She held back her feelings until she could get to her
room. Then she cried.

"But I never want anyone to ever think that I was
an *unclaimed treasure* like Mother was," she whim-
pered to the four walls. *She was so strong, and had to*
be to face the gossip. Even now I can see her brushing her

hair—that luscious brown hair with the blond highlights. It almost seemed as though she was brushing out the filth the town thought about and sometimes even voiced; and brushing off the passes other women's husbands made, thinking she'd be—easy.

Mother would understand. It was just the two of us. Only we knew who my father was. Of course, he knew, but he never even spoke to me or nodded to me when we passed on the street. After him—and me—no one in town would think of marrying Mother.

"Oh!" she sighed, "How she had believed in him!"

Mona, he'll marry me someday—he said so—he said he'll divorce that marshmallow floozy he's married to and marry me and claim you. Mother had said this at least once a week. And she believed it until the day she died.

Mona's anger bubbled up again when she thought about the funeral. *"The closest he got to the sprinkling of people there was the funeral director's office. He sat there huddled down, listening over the loudspeaker, afraid somebody would see him. I was amazed he even came… Mr. McDowell of the McDowell's. I guess you'd have to count him among the mourners.*

Everyone knew the tempo of Father James' prayers, so Mr. McDowell slipped out before the service was over. My only friend, Gerald, saw him. He was just standing around and saw my father's escape.

Dad, Mona wrapped her mind around the thought.

She was jolted out of her memories by a knock on

the door. "Mona! Let's go to the beach! Get your suit on and meet us in the hall!"

As she changed clothes, the familiar fear started again. "Gerald, please put your hand at the small of my back," she whispered and then felt able to put her party face back on. Maybe she'd even have some fun splashing in the waves and building sandcastles, like she and her mother used to do.

Her friends were bubbling as they went down the stairs. "I want one of those big tall pink drinks. You know, one of the pretty ones with the colored straws and the little umbrellas." And off the three of them went.

When Mona woke up the next morning, she felt great. Her back had that gentle warm feeling that just a little too much basking in the sun will bring. The cool, crisp sheets felt so good next to her skin. She fixed herself a cup of coffee and settled back down into the covers again, scrunching her knees up close to her chest. *What fun this trip is! How could I possibly have been afraid of coming?*

She let her mind drift back over the events of the previous day and enjoyed them almost as much in the remembering as she did in the doing. She was looking forward to a trip to the *mercado*. She couldn't wait to see in what decadently outrageous way she was going to splurge on herself. It was getting time to dress. But when she was ready and about to step out the door, the same gnawing knot tensed in the pit of her stomach, "Gerald," she said, "put your hand at the small of my back." She walked out the door.

After a scrumptious brunch of mangos, pineapple, and one or two—too many—of the pastries spread out on the buffet, they walked to the *Mercado*. It was still hot and sultry, but somehow sweating was beginning to seem okay.

The first place they stopped was at a jewelry shop that displayed tray upon tray of beautiful things. The three women tried on what seemed like each one of the pieces of jewelry. One found a pendant with three colors of gold she "couldn't live without!" As an afterthought, as they were headed out the door, Mona decided to have her wedding ring cleaned in one of the electric cleaners she saw on a counter. She indicated to the clerk that was what she wanted. She almost always had her ring cleaned when she went to the mall. It wasn't much of a stone, but it was all she and Gerald could afford at the time. It meant as much to her as the biggest diamond in the world.

When they got ready to leave, Mona opened up her purse to get her sunglasses and scratched her left hand on the clasp. "Ouch!" she screamed, sucking on the small wound. "I've just got to remember to file off that rough spot."

Out in the sun again, the three walked from shop to shop. They looked at leather purses. They tried on embroidered dresses and even had a big bowl of coconut ice cream that had to be loaded with butterfat. It was so-o-o rich and sinfully scrumptious.

Mona finished the last bite. Then she thought the bright sun would probably make the tiny stone in her wedding ring really sparkle. She glanced down and burst into tears. *The stone was gone—vanished!* Her friends huddled around her.

"It's gone!" she gasped, "The stone's gone!" Through the tears she and her friends retraced their steps. "Have you found a small diamond?" Again and again they heard the same response, "No, senora. I'm sorry, but no." They walked back over the route again, looking carefully at each square of sidewalk. Their hopes were raised by the occasional sparkle, which turned out to be only a bit of glass. Back and forth they walked—*nothing!*

Then Mona went back and forth alone until she knew every crack in the sidewalk. Numb, she finally returned to the hotel and locked herself in her room. When she glanced at her left hand, the tears welled up all over again—and again—and again.

She stayed in her room the next day. Her friends knocked on the door and she would say just enough so they knew she was there. Invitations to the beach or to see the ruins always received the same answer, "No, I want to be left alone." Sometimes Mona was eerily still. But her mind was racing, pouring back over her life and even tiptoeing into the future. At intervals, her body's actions would match her mind's racing and she would rock back and forth, clutching her knees tightly to her chest.

Around seven that night she was frantic for something to do with her hands. She remembered the cut on her hand and her vow to file down the rough spot on the clasp. She opened her purse and turned on the bedside lamp. As she reached into the purse to get her reading glasses, she avoided the rough spot on the clasp. She fumbled around in the purse for her glasses. A glint—a tiny sparkle. She kept searching. And there it was again—a tiny glimmer reflected in the lamplight. And then it hit her! She smoothed out the bedspread and dumped the contents of the purse out on the bed. *Nothing!* Then she peered into the purse again. There was a small tear in the lining. No glint! She shook the purse sideways, peered in, and found it—the lost diamond! She let out a squeal of joy and put the small stone in a pillbox in her purse. Then she danced around the room, carefully clutching the special pillbox in her hand. Every now and then, she'd open it up and squeal all over again.

She burst out of the room and banged on her friends' door. "I've found it! I've found it!" she exulted, "Get on your glad rags. I'm taking you two for a night out on the town!"

They ate a grand dinner at the hotel and noticed a room with a dance floor. Each looked at the others and simultaneously said, "Why not!" They made their grand entrance and felt like every eye in the room was on them. A trail of elegant male tourists approached after dinner. When asked for a dance, Mona's reply was, "I'd be delighted!" And at two in the morning, she and her friends finally made it back to their rooms.

Mona waltzed her way back to her room, mimicking the gentlemen dancers. It was hard to sleep, so she decided to pack. She sang and did quick dance steps as she put things into her suitcases. She even pirouetted and bowed to the imaginary gentleman caller in her room.

The next day Mona was still dancing. She walked right up to the desk to settle her bill. "Mona Smith, please, I believe you made an error in the reservation—but no matter. My bill please." After all the checkout formalities were taken care of, Mona told her friends, "I'll hail the cab." She placed two fingers in her mouth and whistled. And a cab whisked up.

There were more details to be taken care of at the airport—the departure tax, baggage check-in, boarding passes—and Mona accomplished each task with the grace and ease of a world traveler. The passport control man was quite short, but Mona walked right up to him and presented her documents with a wave of her hand. She purposefully walked toward the plane, leading the way for her two friends. They looked at each other in astonishment—a new Mona!

❧

Days later, Mona had made up her mind. She got up early and dressed carefully and confidently. "Gerald," she said to herself, "Please put your hand at the small of my back." She couldn't wait to get to the mall and the jewelry store where she always cleaned her rings. She firmly opened the store door and stated, "The jewelry designer, please."

A man walked over, "May I help you?"

With the designer waiting, she carefully opened her purse, unzipped the special compartment, and took out the pillbox. With a faint trace of ceremony, she snapped it open, reached in for its contents and delicately, but purposefully, placed the rings and the small stone on the black velvet pad. "I'd like the gold fashioned as a setting for a pendant, with the single diamond as its central focus." After some discussion the design was decided upon.

From there she drove to the bank. As she approached the doors, she said, "Gerald, please put your hand at the small of my back." With buoyed confidence she walked in. Looking around she found the accounts desk. With a purposeful stride, Mona walked right up to the woman in charge, " I want to change the name on my account. It's now under Mr. or Mrs. Gerald Smith."

"What name do you want to change it to?" the woman asked.

The familiar knot came for the blink of an eye as Mona hesitated. But her indecision was momentary.

"Mona," she had decided on, "M" (for her father's last name) "Smith." I want the account to read Mona M. Smith."

As these words left her mouth, she felt Gerald's hand slowly leave the small of her back.

Jesus said, "Or suppose a woman who has ten silver coins loses one of them, what does she do? She
lights a lamp, sweeps her house, and looks carefully

everywhere until she finds it. When she finds it, she calls her friends and neighbors together, and says to them 'I'm happy! I found the coin I lost! Let's celebrate!'"

Luke 15:8–10 (TEV)

About Shoots And Stumps

Rob's home was nestled in among four acres of timber in East Texas. A medley of pines, oaks, hickory, holly, magnolia and untold other plant species surrounded it. His favorites were the dogwoods that adorned the landscape with delicate white blossoms for a short span in the spring. Originally the acreage had been set aside as a family homestead for a clan who'd owned large stands of timber in the area. Unlike most of the rest of East Texas, this wonderful place had never been harvested; it was one of a very few, old-growth reserves that hadn't been axed. Only in the dead of winter could the house be seen from the road. Even then you had to look real close.

Even today—almost a half century later—Rob's mind's eye revels in the walks he took in those woods as a child. Pines predominated—some so broad even an adult couldn't encircle them with his arms. Sometimes, Rob would look up into their breeze-swaying limbs and couldn't see their tops. Magnolias dotted the landscape, large ones that filled the air with pungent sweetness when white blossoms graced their broad, glossy, dark-green leaves. During Christmas, spiky holly branches gorged with red berries were available for decorating.

But Rob's reverie always focuses on the dogwood that grew outside their dining area window. Large for a dogwood, its blossoms seemed to last longer than any others in the wooded sanctuary. When it bloomed, it was hard for the family to eat and carry on a conversation. Their attention was always drawn to the wonders of the delicate blossoms festooning the tree.

One winter brought a cold snap to top all cold snaps. A giant snowfall blanketed the woods and stayed for weeks. Then a strange, dense fog engulfed everything and froze. For the longest time the temperature hovered way below freezing. The butane lines leading from the tank to the house froze and the family almost had to leave. But Canadian blue Northers can't last forever in East Texas. After several weeks, this one finally left.

The next spring the wonders of the woods began to emerge. Trees that had been so bare sprouted tender new leaves and buds. That is, all of them except the beautiful dogwood outside the dining area window. Each morning Rob and the family would look for new buds, and each morning the family was disappointed.

For them, Spring hadn't officially arrived until that particular dogwood bloomed.

Dad checked again and again, until it became clear that the long cold spell or age itself had killed that beautiful creation. The regal dogwood was gone. Dad cut it down, and made a bonfire out of its branches. The family roasted marshmallows. Even with that pleasant taste in his mouth and the ring of marshmallow goop encircling his lips, Rob still wasn't happy. An old friend was gone.

Later that spring, Rob accompanied Dad doing chores around the place. Their agenda included digging up the roots of the dogwood they'd loved so much. Just as Dad was about to stick the shovel into the ground, Rob shouted and pointed to the ground, "Stop!" A slender, gangly stalk was pushing up in the middle of where the dead wood had been.

Years passed, the sprig grew. Each spring the family noted its progress. Then one special spring they were seated at the table for breakfast. The preserves were being passed around when Mom let out a gasp and pointed. The dogwood had offered up two beautiful blossoms from its slender stalk.

Sometimes now, when Rob is eating by a window, he looks out to see if there's a dogwood blooming outside. And even more, he looks to see if it has sprouted from what people think is a dead stump.

The prophet Isaiah wrote: The royal line of David is like a tree that has been cut down, but just as new branches sprout from a stump, so a new king will arise from among David's descendents. The spirit of the Lord will give him wisdom and the knowledge and skill to rule the people.

Isaiah 11:1–2 (TEV)

Dear James

Listen, James, I'm starting off where I'm supposed to start off. We're told to confront our brothers in love when they've gotten off the track. That's what I'm doing with this letter. The epistle you've been sending around is way out of line. Look! I've got a church to run here and what you wrote is going to take me years to get over. I've worked hard to build up this church and there are folks grumbling about what you say—it will take me forever to get them all mollified. You've done real harm here and I think it's about time you did what you could to undo the mess you've created by writing what you did.

Let me clue you in to the practicalities of church administration. A devoted man who heads up the Property Committee has been working so hard to get our new roof put on. We've had some pretty wealthy people visiting who could pay for that roof with one check and not skip a breath. Are you telling me that they're just as important to the church as those street people who're always lurking around looking for a handout? I think not! When it comes to church budgets I can tell you up front who matters the most—and it's not those people who are too lazy to get a job. It's the outstanding citizens who can work hard and, of course, make a big pledge.

And all that nonsense about where people sit in church. Do you expect me to not ask folks to move when they've sat in a church member's favorite spot in church? There are people who've sat in the same place for over 40 years and I'm not going to disrupt them just because some street urchin wandered in and sat down in the first seat they fancied. It's like reserved seats for a concert. Well, not exactly reserved, but you know what I mean—it's tradition that this one sits here and that one sits there. How else would we know if they were attending if we didn't know where they always sat? Look! Issues like seats are a touchy problem and I don't want to call in any favors just to accommodate some dirty, smelly bum who wouldn't know one seat from another.

Yes, we welcome these people into our church. Well, almost—but we don't make them feel unwanted. It's just that they have to know where their place is. It's part of becoming a member to know who sits where and to avoid that seat. Besides, these people aren't going to join our church, they just wouldn't fit in. And they know it.

About those kids from the housing project—just to show you how open I am, I'll invite them personally to come up for the children's sermon. We won't reject them. After all, we need warm bodies for Sunday School, and they might just start coming. We know that the parents will never be heard from, but that doesn't matter, it's the children's future that counts when it comes to the future of the church. I won't even make the urchins sit in one place apart from the other two church kids.

Now—about that stuff you said about outward appearances. It just doesn't wash today. You might have gotten away with such nonsense back in Jesus' day, but it won't cut it today. People today work long, hard hours to accumulate the things they have. So what if they want to live in a particular part of town? They're willing to work for it. And the poor only take handouts and pester us about low-cost housing and us footing the bill for rooms at the Pelican Inn when they don't pay their bill and get evicted. You think they'd know when the rent was due and plan ahead. A little planning is all they need. But it's always at the last minute—wanting help—and expecting us to pull their chestnuts out of the fire for their lack of thinking ahead.

Look, James, we want people to work hard. You do, too. But there have to be incentives for people to work hard. If there were no prestigious neighborhoods, no luxury cars, no designer clothes, why should they work so hard to earn all that money? In this day and time people who've worked hard to accumulate a few things expect to be treated accordingly. And I'm going to treat them like they expect. How else can we raise all the money for that roof we had to put on. You didn't think of "overhead" when you wrote that drivel about equal places for all.

James, don't you want people to look their best? It costs a lot of money to look good. The bottom would fall out of our economy if people didn't spend what they do on clothes and cars and those sorts of things. After all, there needs to be rewards for people to work hard—that's part of what keeps the economic engine chugging along. Have you seen the stock market over the last year or so? It's gone up several thousand points—yes, several thousand points! The market never would have gone up if these words were taken seriously—you know—the words about how it doesn't matter how you look. After all, rises in the market are how people earn their retirement. Surely you don't have anything against people saving for their golden years.

The worst thing is that junk you wrote that if you broke one commandment you've broken them all. We have a serious crime problem today. It's hard to pick up the newspaper without reading about crime of some sort or another. What deterrent to crime would there be if murders were treated just like tax evasion? The whole fabric of society would break down into moral chaos. How will people know what to do if they aren't told what's right and what's wrong? And, even more important, what's worse behavior and less worse behavior? If everybody got treated just the same, we'd have to turn our homes into fortresses to keep people from breaking into them. And cars—forget them!—they'd be stolen quicker than we could file the insurance claim to get them replaced. James, it's just common sense that some things are worse than others. You know that. And if I let slip with a little "hell," surely I haven't done anything as bad as a murderer or somebody who abducts young girls. And when it comes to sexual matters, we know that those are very important. People today are preoccupied with sex. In order to attract the right people, we have to have some standards about sex matters.

Now, all you've written isn't awful. I feel obliged to find some redeeming qualities about something you've written. That must be somewhere in the Bible. I'm real glad that God does forgive me. I know I couldn't cut the mustard on my own to get my own salvation. Well, I know I won't expend the effort it takes. And I'm glad that God doesn't hold over me the minor slip-ups I make. After all, how important in the big picture is the fact that I fudged on my taxes. I didn't cheat; I just fudged a little bit. And I don't forgive people like I should. Do you remember so-and-so? Yes, you remember what they did to me. It was over 15 years ago, but I still remember. Lord, I've forgiven them, but keep them out of my sight!

Somewhere in the middle, James, you wrote something that disturbs me. You said, "God chose the poor people of this world to be rich in faith and to possess the kingdom promised to those who love him." I know Jesus said the same thing during the Sermon on the Mount, but did you have to say it so bluntly? Those kind of words are going to make it hard to attract the kind of people needed to keep up the budget. If rich folks don't think the Kingdom is an option for them, what's the incentive for them to pay a pledge? Did you think about that when you just randomly picked out of a hat something I'd bet Jesus wishes he could take back!

I'll have to give you this, though, you're right about who you can count on. Boy, will I catch it if I make a blunder with Mrs. So-and-so] She'll make life difficult for me on lots of fronts. You'd think she'd remember all I've done for her. I visited her every day when she was in the hospital—every day—or two weeks. You'd think she'd remember. But when I didn't come see her every day when she got home, all was forgotten.

And that baptism for her neighbor that I rammed through Session. I'm still ashamed of what I said then to get Session to look the other way. And the people never came to "have their baby done" like Mrs. So-and-So said. It wasn't convenient then. Yes, James, you're right: it's the rich folks that have the short memories of the good things you do. It's those poor folks who love me even when I forget to call to "just say hi." It certainly won't be the poor ones talking behind my back and trying to cause trouble just because I slipped up on one small thing.

But James, couldn't you have picked some other quote of Jesus to emphasize? You know, like the one about it's easier for a camel to go through the eye of a needle than for a rich person to get to heaven. No, I guess that's pretty strong, too. And the one about "Go liquidate your assets and give it to the poor." No, that's pretty outrageous, also. There must be something nice Jesus said about people who were concerned about their position in society and worked hard to maintain that position.

Now, here's what I want you to do. Write a letter to the Board that we can publish in the newsletter that says you really didn't mean what you said. That might help me mollify some of the folks who are ticked off. A few personal notes or phone calls would help for some of the more affluent ones. They might be willing to let bygones be bygones. At least, it would make things easier for me. Now, I haven't been all negative about what you said. I did agree with you on one point—the poor don't stab you in the back when you aren't looking.

I've got to go now. There's lots of work to be done to clean up the mess you've made with what you wrote. It will be lots of late nights to get all those bases covered and feathers unruffled.

The more I think about it, the more I realize you're right about the poor not being the ones who hold your feet to the fire. Maybe I'll have to rethink what I've written.

The letter is crumpled up, wadded up, and thrown against a wall.

Dad blast it, he's right! What a muttonhead I've been.

My brothers, as believers in our Lord Jesus Christ, the Lord of glory, you must never treat people in different ways according to their outward appearances. Suppose a rich man wearing a gold ring and fine clothes comes to your meeting, and a poor man in ragged clothes also comes. If you show more respect to the well-dressed man and say to him, "Have this best seat here," but say to the poor man, "Stand over there, or sit here on the floor by my feet," then you are guilty of creating distinctions among yourselves and of making judgments based on evil motives.

Listen, my dear brothers! God chose the poor people of this world to be rich in faith and to possess the kingdom, which he promised to those who love him. But you dishonor the poor! Who are the ones who oppress you and drag you before the judges? The rich! They are the ones who speak evil of that good name which has been given to you.

You will be doing the right thing if you obey the law of the Kingdom, which is found in the scriptures, 'Love your neighbor as you love yourself.' But if you treat people according to their outward appearance, you are guilty of sin, and the Law condemns you as a lawbreaker. Whoever breaks one commandment is guilty of breaking them all. For the same one who said, "Do not commit adultery," also said, "Do not commit murder." Even if you do not commit adultery, you have become a lawbreaker if you commit murder. Speak and act as people who will be judged by the law that sets us free. For God will not show mercy when he judges the person who has not been merciful; but mercy triumphs over judgment.

Epistle of James 2:1–13 (TEV)

Even Dirty Dishes Can Wait

Scene One

The village of Bethany was quiet and peaceful, not at all like Jerusalem, the large city nearby, where there's always some ruckus going on. It's early in what we'd call the first century a.d. It's that time of the day when the heat tends to drive folks indoors where the thick, mud-brick walls make it a little bit cooler. As a side street was neared, the only movement was a couple of dogs battling over a bone that someone's tossed out a window.

But further on down the street there's quite a commotion breaking into the somnolence of the afternoon. It got louder and louder as approached.

"Mary-y-y-y, Mary-y-y-y—He's coming any minute, Mary-y-y, Any minute!"

The home this screech comes from wasn't prepossessing on the outside—just a mud-brick wall with a gate in the middle. Inside the gate, a woman named Martha was bustling about the courtyard frantically. Out loud she's going over a list of things to be done.

"I can't believe we have so little time and so much to do! Let's see, we have the lamb ready and cooking; the dishes are ready and the table's set—and the dates—yes, I think I got those special ones that come from that little stall around the corner. Or did I?" Martha bustles off to check.

"Yes, the dates are there. Oh, no!—the wine—Mary, did you remember to get the wine—you know, that special wine I wanted for company? The one that goes so good with lamb?...Mary?...Are you listening? Oh, I better go see for myself—I'm the only one who gets anything done around this house!" Again Martha bustled off to check on the wine.

She spied Mary. "Did you remember to get that wine I wanted? You know, the one for the lamb? The one we discussed would be just right?"

Serenely, Mary nodded assent. "Yes, I got the wine yesterday. I've already tasted it and it's going to be great. But, if my memory serves me right, it's the wine that *you* chose. I can't recall being consulted about it. Anyway, it's a great choice—and I've got it. Settle down, Jesus won't care what details go into the meal; he just wants to visit us. Remember?

Martha gave her a withering look. "That's easy for you to say. I've been whirring around here getting it all ready and you've just been sitting around. After all, he is the Rabbi!"

About the same time a man was walking down the side street. And can hear the commotion two houses away. He chuckled to himself and shook his head. The sound level escalated so much he feels he had to bang on the gate to get attention. Just as he does, a silence commenced that makes the heavy knocking seem very out of place. But it didn't last for long.

Martha shrieked, "He's here, he's here, and I'm not nearly ready!

Mary opened the gate and let Jesus in, giving and receiving a kiss on the cheek. She bent down to the bowl of water at the gateway—the one that's always kept fresh—and began to wash the dust off Jesus' feet and offered him some fresh sandals to wear indoors. As they entered the home, a jar of olive oil stood by the front door. She dipped her hand in it. Standing on tiptoes she poured the handful of oil over Jesus' head. It trickled down his scalp, some even dripping off his chin.

'Thank you for your hospitality, Mary," Jesus smiled.

Martha hurried out of the back of the house, "Rabbi! Rabbi! How good to see you! Jesus bent down to exchange kisses with her and noticed that her face was clammy with sweat.

"I didn't have time to cool down, Rabbi, there were so many things to get done, and I—didn't—

get—much—help." She glared at Mary who chuckled to herself.

Martha hurried off while Mary invited Jesus to sit down on one of the cushions they have strewn around the room.

"I've been meaning to ask you something, " Mary began. And her deep conversation with Jesus commences. They're quietly talking with each other, but they have to raise their voices to be heard over the commotion going on in the kitchen.

Two rooms away they can hear Martha. "I can't believe her! Dinner is late—there's so much to do, and look at her sitting there as if food appears on the table by waving a magic wand." Then suddenly there's silence from the kitchen. You see, Martha had an idea.

Maybe Jesus can get Mary to help me.

With this thought she rushed out of the kitchen almost breathless, "Jesus, don't you care that *she* has left me to serve alone?"

Jesus patted the cushion next to him and invited Martha to sit down. "Martha, Martha," Jesus said gently grinning at her, "You're all upset and anxious about so many things. But only one thing is important right now. Mary has chosen what's better—and it won't be taken away from her."

Martha looked puzzled and quickly gets up to go back to the kitchen, pausing at the door still trying to sort out what's just been said to her.

Dinner preparations were complete and the three recline on cushions around a low table that was filled with food. Mary and Jesus were still deep in conversation. Several times Jesus triesd to draw Martha into the conversation, but she just mumbled something inaudible and continued eating.

Meanwhile, Mary and Jesus took a break in their conversation and began to eat the feast set before them. After Jesus had eaten heartily, he turned to Martha, "What a wonderful meal you've provided for us. I can't remember having a finer meal!" Mary joined him with her praise

"Humph," was the only answer they get from Martha.

A tale from mid-19th century Africa
Scene two

Natives tell a story about an early missionary who had just arrived by boat from England. He was in a hurry to be about the Lord's business as quickly he could. There were so many souls to be saved and so little time. There was a long trek ahead of him to get to the mission station he'd been assigned to. He contracted with a group of bearers to carry the hoard of supplies he'd brought with him. He was pushing the pace very hard, hoping to cover as much territory each day as possible. But, again and again, he had to backtrack to urge the bearers along.

One morning at the crack of dawn he was up, ready, and raring to go. He stepped out of his tent. "Well, let's get started," he declared.

The bearers were sitting in a circle and ignored him.

"Time's wasting! We have to be on our way. We'll never make the allotment of miles I've set for today if we don't get going."

Again—no response.

He tried ordering them. That didn't work. Then he tried coaxing them. That didn't work. Then he even tried shaming them into action.

No Response!

Finally a bearer spoke up to explain why they wouldn't budge, "We have to stop to let our souls catch up with our bodies."

Celebrating 38, 39 and 40
Scene three

Marissa Langford looks around the Great Room of their home, checking to see that everything is ready for their big celebration party. Her husband, Jackson, is finishing hanging the huge banner over their fireplace. He's having trouble balancing his ladder on the rough flagstone, but finally he tells Marissa, "There it is. It's all hung up! And just in time for our guests to arrive."

As if on cue, the doorbell rings. Georgia and Ralph Larsson are there. Within minutes, twenty other guests appear. There are the usual hugs and greetings. The guests are greeted with quite a display.

Draped over the fireplace that covers one whole end of the room is a huge banner—*Celebrating* 38, 39, *and* 40!

Marissa and Jackson proudly point at the banner. Then they draw their guests' attention to three poster-size photographs adorning the wall adjacent to the large fireplace.

Poster #1 is topped by a banner—*Celebrating* 38. The poster shows a beaming Marissa and Jackson flanking the *Welcome to Utah* sign.

Poster #2's banner reads, *Celebrating* 39. That poster-sized photo depicts a grinning Marissa and Jackson leaning on either side of the *Welcome to Arizona* roadside sign.

Poster #3 announces, *Celebrating* 40. This banner tops a huge portrait of Marissa and Jackson on either side of the *Welcome to Nevada* border announcement.

Jackson gains everyone's attention. "Well, it's official," he boasts with Marissa proudly beaming up at him. "Signed at each visitor center—states number 38, 39, and 40. That's what we got done on this year's vacation. Isn't it great?" Sporadic applause responds to his announcement. "Next year we have plans for 41, and 42 and possibly 43 if things work out. In three years we'll have accomplished it! *Being in all* 50 *states!*

A few tepid congratulatory comments diminish Jackson's beam some, but quickly the pride of his accomplishment resurfaces.

After the grand announcement is over, the guests are invited to partake of the refreshments that crowd an extended dining room table. They find this much more interesting and commence eating their fill of all the goodies.

Miranda Schmidt corners Marissa, "What did you think of Monument Valley? We were there two years ago and were awestruck by the columns standing out in the middle of nowhere that nature had fashioned. That's where movie director John Ford shot *stagecoach*. It's near one of those atomic proving grounds. That's a shame. John Wayne and Susan Hayward were in a movie about Genghis Khan that was made there. Did you know that they both died of cancer? In fact, an alarming number of actors and others working on the picture died of cancer. I've always wondered if it was because of the atomic proving grounds.

Marissa's face gets a quizzical look, "Monument Valley? Monument Valley? I vaguely remember glancing at some strange rock formations, but I had to do my *map duty*. Jackson was afraid that we wouldn't make it to Arizona while the welcome center was still open. He wanted me to keep him posted on how far we had to go, giving regular updates. You see, I'm the official navigator on our trips. And it was important for me to make sure how far it was to the center. We wouldn't want to miss that, and we weren't quite sure what time zone we were in—it changes because of the Navajos who want daylight saving time and the state of Arizona that doesn't. But we made it!" she accented with a *high-five* with her husband who'd joined her. "It turned out we had an hour to spare. But we weren't sure."

Later in the evening, Burt Cranston hails Jackson from across the room and starts heading over to him as he asks, "Hey, guy, what did you think of the Grand Canyon? Jackie and I sat on a bench right at the edge of the canyon and watched the most incredible sunset.

You wouldn't believe how vivid the colors were. And the hues the canyon turned as the sun left them in darkness. I don't think I've ever seen a more beautiful dark purple than I did on the canyon side as the sun set. We must have stayed there two hours or so. We didn't realize how long we'd sat there until our stomachs started grumbling for their supper. Jackie fished around in her purse for some crackers she had stashed away. We nibbled on them to quiet our stomachs long enough to see the final moment of the sunset.

"Ah—Grand Canyon—that must have been something." Jackson looks around the room, then down at his shoes, "We never made it to Grand Canyon. There was a lot of construction on the road. They'd closed one lane so we had to wait for a long time to get our chance to go down the open lane. We saw the sign for Grand Canyon and almost turned in to get a quick look, but the Nevada Welcome Center closed at five and we were afraid we wouldn't make it in time. In fact, they were locking the doors as we pulled up. But we talked them into re-opening to sign our book to prove we'd been in Nevada.

Burt walked away shaking his head in mystification.

"But we did get it signed," Jackson beamed. "See, over there?"

Even Dirty Dishes Can Wait
Scene Four

The family night supper at the church had just fin-

123

ished. Folks were gathered around talking, enjoying each other's company and commenting on the slide show of the Holy Land they'd seen and the good food the potluck had.

"I'm so stuffed, I don't think I'll want to eat for another week," Ben commented, patting his distended middle.

On the other side of the room Nancy was quizzing a group of women. "Who made the rum chocolate cake? I could smell the rum as a family brought it in. I don't know their names, but you remember the woman in the wheelchair? I just had to get a slice of it. Wow, it was scrumptious! And you sure could taste the rum. I almost got a buzz from the two slices I ate."

"I didn't get any," Amy complained. It was gone by the time it was my turn in the line. I think it was all gone before a third of the folks had passed by. I know that family. They're the Elliott's, Ben, Eve and Ricky. Eve's the one in the wheelchair. I'll go see if I can get the recipe from her."

Nancy's group watched as Eve was approached. They noticed Eve shake her head from side to side and point to her boy.

Amy returned to the gaggle of women. "You're not going to believe the story. Her son made it. There wasn't any rum extract, so he raided the liquor cabinet for the real thing. He thought the rum in the bottle was about half as thick as the other extracts, so he used twice as much of the rum. Then the rum bottle slipped when he was making the icing, but there wasn't time, so…"

They all got a good laugh. Then Gloria came over to them. I need help clearing the dishes. Then she got on the PA system and announced, "Men, we need those tables broken down after the ladies clear them off. Let's get going, ladies, so the men can get their job done." The announcement wasn't heeded and folks continued visiting with each other. Finally, Gloria collared a group of ladies and pointed each to a table. "Get that one cleared, then come help us get things in the dishwasher." After the dishes finally made it into the kitchen, Gloria haggardly yelled orders at some men. "We need those tables broken down and put away. Let's not take all night."

Mary Goodson, the church matriarch, tried to catch Gloria's eye, but was unsuccessful. She spoke to a young girl sitting next to her and stood up with some difficulty, wobbling until she could get her walker. Laboriously she moved toward the kitchen. At the door she stopped to catch her breath and tried to get Gloria's attention. She walked over to one place, but by the time she and her walker got there, Gloria had moved to another area of the kitchen. Finally she got one of the women to bring Gloria to her.

Wiping her hands on her apron, Gloria walked over to Mary. "I think we have things in hand. You don't need to put yourself out to help us."

Gloria was about to walk away when Mary said, "That's not what I wanted you for. I want you to meet my great-granddaughter. You know, the one who was named for me. We've been such good friends over the years, and I just wanted you to see her. She's here from California and is leaving tomorrow morning. Heaven knows when I can talk them into bringing her back for a visit."

Walking away, Gloria turned and said, "I'll be right out after I've got this kitchen crew going. There're so many dishes to be done, and somebody left the coffee urns on after they were empty and they got scorched. Give me a minute, and I'll be right out."

Mary walked slowly back to her companion. "There's this close friend I want to meet you. We've known each other for so long. I've shown her your pictures, but I want you to meet this special lady face to face."

Ten minutes passed. Mary tried to see how the kitchen progress was going. Gloria popped her head out after fifteen minutes to announce, "Just a little while longer." Meanwhile, the child was beginning to fidget. "I'm sleepy, Grans, I want to go back to your house."

"Just a little while more, it won't take long—and this will probably be the only time you'll get to meet my friend because your folks are going overseas."

A half hour had passed and the child was starting to get antsy. "I want to go, Grans! Now!"

After five more minutes and no Gloria, Mary said, "Fetch my walker, sweetie." She took one last look at the frantic activity in the kitchen and began to slowly walk out the door. The look of disappointment creased her face.

After another ten minutes, Gloria came out of the kitchen, took a quick look around and saw that no one was there. She felt a twinge of guilt then chased it away with *But we'd never gotten things cleaned up if I hadn't been there.*

Martha was upset over all the work she had to do, so she came and said, "Lord, don't you care that my sister has left me to do all the work by myself? Tell her to come and help me!"

The Lord answered her, "Martha, Martha! You are worried and troubled over so many things, but just one is needed. Mary has chosen the right thing and it will not be taken away from her."

Luke 10: 40–42 (TEV)

Communal Living in the Early Church, Part 1

Jane stands in the middle the family room and slowly turns. Jane is a regal woman, barely five feet tall. "Five foot two," she always answered. Her back is straight, her head erect. She's nicely dressed, even wearing the dainty string of pearls that belonged to her great grandmother. Her chin is slightly lifted in the posture the finishing school had taught her was appropriate for ladies of substance.

Her chin stops turning and she stares at one corner of the room. *That's where we always put the Christmas tree.*

Another turn. *And that's where Carol was sitting when Jack proposed. We were huddled in the living room anxiously waiting for the event Jack had let slip.*

Another turn reveals a big, overstuffed recliner

nestled between two side tables that were once covered with papers and magazines and all the stuff Brad needed when he worked at home. *And that's where I found him dead that awful morning.* She feels the shock and sadness. The familiar catch in her throat comes again. *You'd think I'd be over his death after all these years.*

She continues slowly turning. Her slow inspection of the room that bursts with so many happy memories.

Then she lifts herself out of her reverie, remembering that that was then and this was now. She involuntarily gasps as she remembers the reason for looking this room over. Her indecision returns. *After forty years in this beautiful home in California, maybe it's time to leave.*

I remember, she reminisces, *how Brad and I stumbled across this beautiful mission-style house on a quiet street. We knew right off that it had to be our home. I can still feel the panicky moment when we heard the price. It was going to stretch our family resources to the limit. The only way we could even consider it was because it badly needed renovation.*

A faint smile caresses the corners of her mouth, recalling those renovations, *every member of the family was involved, picking out the curtains, the carpet, and the paint colors. Each daughter was allowed to choose the color and curtains for her own room.* Jane rubs the small of her back, feeling for a moment the catch in her back she got while painting the living room ceiling—*so long ago.*

An earth tremor shakes her out of her memories.

Anyway the kids are long gone. I've been alone here for fifteen years now, and it just doesn't make sense keeping all this space for the occasional time when the whole family gets together for a holiday.

Another tremor hits. She's been feeling tremors all morning. She reminds herself, *that's just part of living in California.*

She keeps recalling all the headaches that went along with this old house. It was always something. If it wasn't keeping good yard help, it was the trips upstairs to check out how everything was doing. *That's the only time I ever go upstairs and there's always something that needs fixing, or changing, or adjusting. And it takes forever to get somebody out to do what needs doing. Remember how your knees ache for days and how breathless you feel climbing those stairs.* She feels the beginnings of a headache just thinking about it. With a forced look of determination she realizes, *I've got to move!*

What she's really bothered about is going through the accumulation of *things*—each one with a memory attached. She begins in the kitchen, thinking it would be the easiest. She opens a drawer and sifts through its contents. In drawer after drawer she looks at the gadgets, lifts one up as something she might give away, but it soon becomes like the chorus of a song, *I might need that.*

Hopefully she goes to the storage closet and stumbles across a box she can't quite place. She opens it and the contents are still *store-wrapped* though discolored with age. A card is neatly placed on top. It's a wedding present they'd never used. But it goes on the *to keep* list because of the warm feelings she has when she remembers the people who had given it.

Another tremor.

From room to room she moves. In each the story is the same: she just can't let go of *that*—it was so special, in spite of the fact she hadn't used it in more years than she could count. After covering each room and making some notes, she returns to the family room.

She feels a stronger tremor.

A little breathless from the exertion, she sits down on a sofa and takes an inventory of all those things to keep. She knows what she *needs*—well, really to be truthful—what she *wants* to keep. As she reviews her list, she realizes that she would need a place at least this big to keep it all.

"I might as well stay in this one," she affirms tentatively.

Then the earth releases a stronger jolt. Something crashes down in the kitchen. She goes to check on it and decides to turn on TV to see if there are any news reports about the earth tremors she's been feeling. What she beholds twists a knot in the pit of her stomach: horrendous devastation wrought by a major earthquake a hundred miles away. It's a horrible scene: houses collapsed, gas lines burning, cars upended, tall office buildings pancaked, with glass and debris everywhere. The horror scene is still in her mind as she picks up the picture that was shaken off the wall.

It is a picture called *Grace,* depicting an old man

with creases lining his face and forehead. He has raised his work-gnarled hands and clasped them together in prayer, resting his elbows on the table. In front of him is a loaf of bread, knife lying ready, and a bowl probably containing soup or a savory stew. He's taken off his spectacles and laid them on a thick bible.

The picture reminds Jane of the rich life she's lived—a loving husband, two children who still think to call her every two weeks, and the plethora of memories that accompany the tear that rolls down her cheek. Suddenly she feels very old and left behind, but wants to cling to the abundance of things that others would consider only clutter. She stares at the picture once again as she re-hangs it in the place where it's been for forty years. Suddenly the picture relates to her what she needs to do.

She sits at her kitchen table and begins to pray. Her talk with God commences with a jumble of thoughts—giving thanks, yet reprimanding God for leaving her alone with only a smattering of the old friends she's shared her life with. Then she remembers that this prayer is to be asking God what she needs to do about this house and all the pile of *things* it holds

Then the news anchor disturbs her meditation. "What people need now are basic necessities to get started again—dishes, furniture, clothes, the little things to set up housekeeping with."

It hits her! Her determined jaw announces that she has a plan that needs to be put into action with great dispatch.

Jane goes next door to her neighbor who drives the big moving van that people always complain about being parked on the street.

"I need you and your truck," she announces to the stunned owner. "We need to get things moving. Help me get the neighbors. You go that way and I'll go this way."

Shaking his head in bemusement, the trucker does as he's told because the determined look her family knew so well let him know that she'd brook no arguments. Purposefully she strides off. She stops people she sees outside, kids coming home from school, anybody she thinks can lift even a light load. Her authoritativeness gathers a gaggle of people. Before long a steady stream is moving in her kitchen door and out her living room door. Jane supervises each room in a manner any drill sergeant would have envied. Like ants, they take off load after load of the precious things she, only recently, had thought she could never part with. Onto the truck they go. When the truck is full, it moves off and comes back empty. By then another load is stacked up, ready to leave.

It's almost midnight before the stream of humans complete their work. She takes a moment to look around her house. All that's left is a favorite sofa and chair, her new refrigerator, her own bedroom furniture, a small dinette set and some clothes—only the ones that she'd worn within the last two years.

"That'll be all I really need in my new apartment,"

she affirms to herself. She doesn't have a single qualm. A big smile crosses her face.

> And Luke tells us, "No one said that any of his belongings was his own, but they all shared with each other everything they had...There was no one who was in need. Those who owned fields or houses would sell them, bring the money received from the sale...and the money was distributed to each one according to his need."
>
> Acts of the Apostles 4:32–35 (TEV)

Communal Living in the Early Church, Part II

It was a quiet Sunday morning. There wasn't much movement in the disheveled neighborhood. Hulks of cars lined the street. All of them looked like they were held together with bailing wire and bubble gum. Ancient oil stains blotched the sides of the street. In several driveways cars stood on blocks, their license plates years out of date. Houses—ones that looked like they'd been built in the post-WWII building boom—lined the street, each one just like the next. The only thing that individualized them was the state of disrepair. Many had screens hanging loose on rusted-out hinges that had given way. Others showed long years of needing to be painted. Occasionally, there'd be one that was fixed up. Those usually were painted in gaudy colors.

Two imposing edifices book-ended the street. One was a warren of closely built apartment buildings. Clotheslines draped the backyards—a curiosity from a bygone era, but still in full use here. *Amber Lakes Village,* a dilapidated sign announced. Though one would have to imply that since many of the letters had been shot out or painted over with graffiti.

The other edifice was a soaring gothic church. Bold, ornate letters proclaimed the name of the congregation. A parking lot abutted the church building, not church. In neat rows, with many spaces vacant, well-maintained cars were parked. New ones. Almost new ones. None in need of paint. No petroleum detritus was in evidence. The lawns were neatly and tastefully landscaped. One could envision postcard perfection. A faint sound of organ music and people singing wafted out of the building. Harvest decorations tastefully adorned the doors of the church.

The inside of the sanctuary mirrored the grandeur of the exterior. A sprinkling of people filled the huge hall. Velvet ropes blocked off the back pews, though some of them had been removed and occupied. Canned goods, foodstuffs, household necessities draped the places where flowers normally would have been.

Ushers stood at the front of the sanctuary, offering plates having been just handed to them. As they were turning to take the collection, sirens and claxons of emergency vehicles passing in front of the building hardly caused a second glance. Nobody thought much about it since almost no one in the congregation still lived in the neighborhood anymore. The meditative music of the offertory modulated into the majestic chords of the Doxology. The first scent of smoke wafted in. The minister prayed over the receipts. More smoke was detected, even causing some heads to turn.

"Now, we're going to take our second offering," the minister intoned. "You see the things gathered on previous Sundays this month. We all need to be generous." The smoke billowed into the sanctuary. "Jack, please see what's happening," the minister said. Quiet descended over the worshippers. Heads turned around. Then speculation concerning the cause of the fire began to be whispered throughout the throng.

Jack returned to breathlessly announce, "The projects are on fire. We'd better get the hoses out and douse the roof to keep it from catching, too."

A group of men rushed out the back door of the church. They were hauling out the hoses, when one noticed, "Looks like the flames are subsiding." The others looked too and agreed.

"Let's watch for a while with the hoses ready in case it flares up again. The flames were still licking out of some of the windows they could see. Then they noticed the crowd slowly approaching. There were children, parents, old folks—all trudging along. A few clutched meager possessions, but most were empty-handed. On they came.

"Over here!" one of the guys yelled, "Over here! Come on inside. There's room for everybody." The pace of the throng picked up a little as they headed for the church.

A side door into the fellowship hall was held open by one man and in came hordes of people. But none of them uttered a word. Silently they trudged in. Several looked from side to side as though they didn't belong. But they were quickly encouraged to enter.

Meanwhile, in the sanctuary, worship had ceased. The second offering—food stuffs like those being used to decorate the altar. One purposeful woman stood and called out, "Food committee, we need to go downstairs!" And a coterie of folks rushed down to the fellowship hall.

For an instant the rest were in kind of a daze. Then it struck them individually. One after another they walked out of the church. Usually folks lingered to visit, but not today. Intently, they reached their cars and drove away, dodging the throng slowly coming into the church.

In the grocery store nearby a church member said to another, "Fancy meeting you here. Here to do your shopping? I thought I'd get a few things to bring back to help those folks out."

"Me too," was the answer. The church folks kept bumping into friends, each with a cart loaded up. Then the checkout lanes rowed up. The manager, with a befuddled look on his face, summoned more clerks to handle the crowd that was backing up. "I've never had this many folks at this time," he mused, shaking his head from side to side. Then he joined the clerks to check the folks out. The meager group of sackers was completely overwhelmed so volunteer customers joined those who packed the merchandize and food purchased.

The caravan of cars returned to the parking lot and folks burdened with things came into the sanctuary and placed their purchases at the front of the church. It wasn't long before the altar area was overflowing with food. Next, the front pews were piled high with food, clothing, and all sorts of things. By the time the last of the new purchases had been placed, the front half of the sanctuary was piled high with goods. They headed for the fellowship hall after they'd deposited their goods.

Downstairs, the Food Committee was busily at work. A covered dish luncheon celebrating Thanksgiving had been scheduled. No one had questioned what to do with the groaning board of food there. Quickly, food was warmed, arranged, and ready to serve. There was turkey, dressing, multiple different green bean casseroles, salads, congealed salads, fresh baked rolls, cakes, cookies, pies and lots more. When all was ready, the chairwoman went out to a family and invited them to serve themselves.

"No, that's your food," the woman with four children clutching her skirt replied.

"I invited you," was the reply, "and everyone." She kept beckoning with welcoming waves. One by one the people lined up, took a china plate and were served. The tables had been decorated festively with seasonal items. There were Pilgrim pictures on the placemats, and shiny flatware. Glasses were filled with the cranberry tea that was the specialty of one of the committee members.

The first family served hesitantly took forks from the place settings and began to eat standing up. The committee chairwoman ushered them over to one of the tables and indicated they should be seated. Hesitantly, they took their place, followed by others. And before long, conversation, even a hesitant laugh or two, filled the room.

"Come back for seconds! There's plenty. And don't forget dessert. We've got enough sweet stuff here to keep a city of dentists occupied."

The recently redecorated fellowship hall soon smelled like smoke and stale sweat, but no one took notice. The church folks stood among the tables visiting with the burned out throng, sometimes helping get refills of tea or a fresh plate of cookies. But none of the congregation members ate. When the last visitor in line had been served, there was little hesitation in returning for second helpings.

By this time kids were racing up and down the aisles playing make-up games. Occasionally, one would be admonished, but activity was resumed minutes later. And the din recommenced. Things quieted down when the minister stood. "We almost forgot something. Let's bless this food by singing the Doxology together. After you've finished, please come up to the sanctuary. There are some things we want you to have."

With tentative steps, one person after another ventured up the steps to the sanctuary. Upon entering all eyes focused on the cornucopia of things assembled there. Sacks and bags and boxes were handed out and the people began to make their selections.

Meanwhile, downstairs, a group of teenagers quickly broke down the tables while the dishwashers hummed. The church folks, gathered in the sanctuary, began picking up pew cushions and carried them down to the fellowship hall. They were laid along the walls and in rows with chairs interspersed.

The fire victims were about to head out the front door of the sanctuary, each laden with bags and sacks and boxes full of necessities. "Wait a moment," a church member called out. "Come back to the fellowship hall. There's no place for you to go. We've got it set up as a temporary shelter until other arrangements are made."

Already overwhelmed by the meal and the items they'd selected from the sanctuary, some began to cry—a mixture of loss, relief and a bevy of roller coaster emotions.

And there they stayed for several days until temporary housing had been arranged. Groups from the church volunteered to provide meals. By the second day, all the folks—church members and burned out victims—were intermingled as they worked to get the meals prepared. Bathroom and shower facilities were a bit haphazard and overtaxed, but no one seemed to care.

As the last of the people had left, one woman noticed a sign that had been tacked to a wall after the refurbishing had taken place. "Room Use Policies," it read. With a chuckle she tore it down and continued her clean-up work.

Luke writes,

"No one said that any of his belongings was his own, but they all shared with each other everything they had...There was no one who was in need. Those who owned fields or houses would sell them, bring the money received from the sale, and the money was distributed to each one according to his need" (Acts of the Apostles 4:32–35, TEV).

Be Still And Know That I am God

Roxanne had to *get outta Dodge!* Tired, out of sorts, frustrated, and bored—she definitely had to *get outta Dodge!* It wasn't anything anybody did especially, she just had to go.

An accumulation of little things had piled up. People hadn't done what they said they'd do, yet they were blaming her for the job not getting done (or at least she was imagining they were). A nagging cough—maybe a cold—was dragging her down, but she didn't feel she had the time to kick back and rest to help it go away. She was bad about that, and her body suffered for it. She knew she needed to let up a little, but didn't. So sometimes the *ole bod* finally had had enough and it would grind her to a halt.

Roxanne would keep attempting to get things done, but she'd feel like she was trying to corner Jell-

145

O™ with a hot fork. Finally, this time, she gave in to the need to get away, and she went.

After church services, she took the convertible top off her car even though it was a little cool and rain was threatening. But with a challenging glower at the sky and a flick of the switch, she was on her way. Houston traffic was awful—even for a weekday, and here it was a Sunday. No matter which lane Roxanne tried, there was a slow-up, a wreck, a bottleneck, or folks lollygagging at other people's misfortune on the lanes going in the opposite direction. Roxanne fidgeted in the seat, finger-typed on the steering wheel, and came close to making obscene gestures at folks who slowed her progress.

The first night the bed was hard, the pillows flat, and the compressor on the air-conditioner sounded like a diesel engine every time it cycled on.

The next day was spent meandering through a marvelous, wild animal park. While watching a herd of dik-dik, she suddenly felt a tap-tap-tap on the top of her head. She turned and looked up, straight into the eyes of an ostrich. Apparently the beast wanted a handout, but it backed off quickly when Roxanne glowered at it.

Later, as she traveled north, a truck tried to run her off the road. So she wasted precious vacation hours in the local sheriff's office in hopes that the law would make the offending truck driver feel the full brunt of her righteous indignation. It didn't work.

After a better night's rest featuring softer pillows and no air-conditioning noise, she whizzed through breathtaking Palo Duro Canyon. She hardly saw a thing and then got angry at herself when she slipped in the mud and got her clothes all yucky. *Why—when it hardly ever rains in this part of the country—did it have to rain now so I could slip in the mud and lose my dignity?* She still could hear the laughter of the hikers on the path nearby.

The following night was spent in a chain motel in Amarillo. Roxanne had a momentary feeling of victory when the price of the night's stay was quite reasonable for the room she got. But, in the middle of the night, she stumbled out of bed and fell on the floor. She stood back up and immediately fell on her face again. After several abortive attempts at staying erect, she reluctantly gave in. She just couldn't stand up. So she crawled to the bathroom on her hands and knees. To her chagrin, she soon discovered that vertigo and her usual way of accomplishing these late night tasks was not compatible. Needless to say, she was frightened. The *feeling sorry for myself* syndrome took over. Here she was, sick on her vacation, in a strange place, and in a rented room to boot. *Why me?* Roxanne raged. *Why is it always me?*

The next morning she called the front desk to inquire about medical facilities. The lady who answered had a kind voice and, after Roxanne described her problem, the woman sent her son to help Roxanne get to the doctor. And so, with a teenager propping her up, and a queasy stomach that could have been menacing if it contained anything, she hobbled into the doctor's office. Yep, an inner ear affliction.

Roxanne had considered all sorts of dire maladies, so she was somewhat relieved to hear her problem was something simple. With a full bottle of Antivert in hand, back she went to the motel. The kid was really enjoying driving the little sports car. There were a few anxious moments for the passenger, but he got her where she needed to go and back.

Back in the room, she popped a few pills, ordered in some pizza, and slept most of the day. By evening she was feeling well enough to make a foray out of the room. The Italian restaurant right across the street carried Italian gelato ice cream on the menu. She didn't have the vaguest notion where to get gelato in Houston, yet found it in the wilds of Amarillo.

The next day was glorious. Fortified with pills, Roxanne found a great doughnut shop a block from her motel. The coffee was full-bodied and the jelly doughnuts were so full it was difficult to keep them from oozing all over her fingers. She found a stretch of road north of Amarillo that was actually scenic compared to the flat sameness of the High Plains. In New Mexico, she toured an extinct volcano. From atop the volcano she could make out the lava flows and wondered what the terrain was like when the earth used this spot to spew its scalding guts from deep below.

Finally, she crossed into her destination—Colorado. A helpful lady in the tourist information office recommended several spectacularly beautiful dirt-road drives through the Rockies. They lived up to their billing. Then she took the cog-wheel train to the top of Pike's Peak. It was snowing; something she hardly ever got to see in sub-tropical Houston. Instead of enjoying the novelty of the white flakes, she was grumpy because she hadn't brought a jacket.

When she got back to the car, it wouldn't start. She'd left the lights on and the battery had run down. She was glad church folks weren't there to hear the oaths she hurled to the heavens. Then, out of nowhere, four husky young men appeared. They picked up her car and turned it around so she could roll down an incline and pop the clutch. She thanked them off-handedly and they went on their way.

Rocky Mountain Park made her aware of her mortality. At that elevation, it took her a half-hour to walk a short distance to what was supposed to be a spectacular vista. She was so caught up in her breath-ing, she only summarily scanned the scenery before huffing and puffing back to the car. This was the first occasion she had contemplated going home. But, since she was bound and determined to have a good time, she vowed to *stay the course*.

Roxanne tried out another of the dirt-road treks recommended to her. It was spectacular in a differ-ent way; strange rock formations were on either side. They looked like some celestial child had strewn them around like marbles. Then a few winces in her upper jaw caught her attention—especially when the car bounced over bumps in the road. It wasn't long before the winces turned into full-fledged throbbing in Roxanne's ears. Beautiful rock formations passed by, but all she could think was, *I'm going to die.* The throbbing was so bad she contemplated screaming, and probably would have if there had been anyone around to hear her.

Fortuitously, at the intersection where the dirt road ended, a small-town hospital appeared. The diagnosis was a pedestrian ear infection. However, the doctor was concerned and insisted this tourist must stay at a local motel for the night, "Just in case." He mentioned something about eardrum ruptures, but Roxanne only focused on the eardrops he said would handle the pain. Those miraculous drops made the hurt go away. After a shot in the rump and a prescription, the doctor sent her on her way.

Then an event that city dwellers would marvel at— the pharmacy Roxanne went to didn't take charge cards. She was delightfully flabbergasted when the pharmacist said, as if this were no matter of great concern, "We'll take a check." Roxanne walked out of the pharmacy, prescription in hand, with a mouth dropped so wide open she could have swallowed swarms of mosquitoes.

The only motel in town was homey with window boxes full of flowers adorning each room. Roxanne was just settling down for the night when the phone rang. The doctor was calling to check on her! She wondered how he knew where she was, but then remembered there was only one motel, so his detective skills weren't challenged too much. There couldn't be too many crazy Texans in a sports car meant for teenagers in that small town that night. Some part of her yearned to live in such an atmosphere of trust and caring.

The next morning she was feeling some better, but her spirits were still low. She vacillated as she tried to decide whether she would head for home early or not. Some aberrant strain of the Calvinistic work ethic caused her to forge on. The vacation she'd laid out was still waiting to be completed. She was no quitter, so her vow to finish the task—no matter what—was reaffirmed and, with firm purpose, she drove on.

Grumbling along mountain roads, she muttered about the horrible condition of the highways—*Colorado sure did need to get its act together.* Occasionally she glanced up to see some sights. *They're nice all right,* she thought, *but it's taking most of my attention to avoid the potholes.* She decided to cut the Colorado Highway Authority some slack, allowing as how rough winters would make it difficult to keep the roads up. But, then she countered, *Why do they have to be so slovenly on the highway I'm traveling on.* In short, Roxanne was enjoying a first-class, pity-party to which she was the only one invited.

Suddenly, a violent thunderstorm that seemed to come out of nowhere caught her with the convertible top down. It took quite a feat of speed and dexterity to get the top on before everything, including Roxanne, got drenched. She was partially successful, getting only moderately wet. The interior of the car got just wet enough to make small, mud splotches where dust had reigned. The rain poured down in sheets. Streaks of lightning sparked all around. The car even rocked gently from the winds. By now the pity-party was in full swing. Then, as abruptly as it had come, the rain stopped and the sky cleared to that ice blue you can see only in the mountains.

Only then did she notice the aspen trees on a mountainside. The storm winds were still blowing in their elevation, so they were rippling the trees back and forth. The colors were gently changing from summer pale green to fall's hues of gold. Roxanne marveled at the sight as she pulled over and sat transfixed, soaking in the swaying changes of the iridescent hues.

Then, above the mountain, a complete double rainbow formed. The colors were vivid and defined—nothing like the washed out, incomplete colors she was accustomed to in Texas. And deep inside her a voice gently spoke. *"Be still—and know that I am God."*

Suddenly, there was a breathtaking sharpness to her sight. She could clearly see the wonders of God's creation. The silence seemed to sweep away the detritus that had so cluttered her life. She hadn't been able to ecognize that God had been caring for her all along. The Creator had sent many people into her life. They had gone unrecognized as God, until that moment of stillness. She even revisited, in her mind's eye, the places where she'd just blindly been and now was able to revel in their full majesty.

"Be still," God says, "and know that I am God, supreme among the nations, supreme over all the world"

Psalm 46:10 (personal paraphrase)

The Lord Almighty is with us; the God of Jacob is our refuge.

Psalm 46:11 (TEV)

The Search Committee

You should have seen the rain pouring down on Prestige Protestant Church in suburban Houston. It was coming down in sheets. And the lightning—it was crackling like hot power lines. But, inside, the church was dry and a committee was hard at work. The folks had been charged with the important task of nominating one member of the congregation to receive the Church Member of the Year award. They were concentrating on their work so hard they didn't even hear or see nature's pyrotechnics.

John Bankwell spoke in his resonating baritone voice. "As chairman of the Finance Committee, I think we should choose Bill Buckston as Church Member of the Year!" he announced. "I can personally bear testimony, since I handle the deposits every Sunday and audit the books that we couldn't possibly do without Bill. He's far and above the biggest contributor to our church. Nobody even comes close." Bankwell nodded with finality as though the decision already had been made and agreed upon.

"But he doesn't come to church except at Easter and Christmas," a committee member observed, "and he never does anything to help out around here."

"That's because he's so busy managing his assets," Bankwell assured them. "Every civic club in town has honored Bill with their highest service award. It's time we recognized his important contribution to our congregation. It couldn't hurt. After all, we've been running a bit short of late. We know we always can turn to Bill if we run into a rough financial patch and need some tiding-over help. The Finance Committee is just about at that point now, in fact. So it would be a good time to name Bill Buckston as Church Member of the Year." He again nodded with finality to indicate that he thought the issue was settled.

Janice Patrick jumped into the lull in the conversation. "I think we should pick Nancy Gardiner as Church Member of the Year. We all know what she does for the church grounds. She must be up here every day, down on her hands and knees, planting, pruning, moving plants from one place to another. Why, everybody knows we have the prettiest churchyard in town. And it would look just awful if Nancy Gardener didn't put in so much work. People are attracted to a church by how it looks, so Nancy's work is about the best evangelism tool we could have. And it doesn't hurt any that we win Yard Beautiful every year in the

Church and Business category. That picture in the paper brings in lots of people. Why, I notice it every year and look forward to seeing it."

Janice had barely looked around to see if there was agreement before somebody else on the committee chimed in, "I think it's time we recognized Granny Morgan. She's been in this church for over 80 years and hasn't missed a Sunday unless she was sick or visiting family. She's been teaching the Philathea Class—you know, the old ladies class—for as long as people can remember. That, in itself, should bring her the honor. It must be hard to keep that deaf bunch awake and not talking about bunions, arthritis, angina, shingles and any other malady of the day."

Another voice piped in, "But she just reads the lesson from the leaflet, and she doesn't even do that very well. Yeah, it's great she's been around for that long, but how does just hanging around qualify anyone to be Church Member of the Year?"

"Besides," John Bankwell interrupted, "she only puts a quarter in the plate every Sunday. Only a quarter! Eighty years ago that would have amounted to something, but not today. It doesn't even pay for the utilities it takes to keep her old bones warm. We really ought to consider Bill Buckston. After all..."

A voice breaks in, "I know! Let's honor one of the high-school kids who are graduating. Sherry Dancer would be a great choice. She's been Student Council president, a member of the Honor Society, and a cheerleader. Just her being at Youth Group guarantees there'll be a bevy of boys there."

"Yeah, but she comes in for worship and sneaks out when the sermon starts so she can get a head start on the punch before everybody else."

A chorus of other complaints about Sherry Dancer erupted, until a loud clap of thunder crackled outside. And the lights went out!

Somebody thought they smelled something electrical burning, but couldn't see any smoke.

'What are we going to do?" it seemed everybody howled at once.

A voice timidly suggested, "I'll bet Jim Wire would come. You know Jim—he sits with his family on the third pew from the front on the right side." Recognition came with a chorus of *Oh, yeahs.* That was easy to recall since almost nobody sits near the front. So Jim was called as soon as someone could feel their way to a phone. One man stumbled over a chair and fell, but didn't damage anything serious—just his pride.

"Hello," Jim Wire said as he answered his phone. "It's who? Oh yeah, I know you, from church...You say you think there might be something electrical burning?...Uh-huh. Uh-huh...You'd better check all the rooms to see. Meanwhile, I'll come right over. But check all the rooms. It'll save me time. If there really is a fire, call 911...Yeah, yeah...good-bye...uh-huh, uh-huh...See you soon." Jim hung up before another chorus of possibilities flooded the phone line.

In spite of the dark, members of the committee exchanged glances, the lightning supplying just enough light.

"Maybe we ought to make Jim Wire Church Member of the Year. He's always there when somebody calls with a problem with the electricity at the church. And he doesn't charge," a committee member offered.

"Heaven knows," John Bankwell opined, "how much it would cost us to pay for an electrician. The wiring in this place is only a couple generations younger than Noah's Ark. That's a splendid idea! If we can't choose Bill Buckston, John Wire would be a great nominee. The Finance Committee would certainly approve. But we'd better get about looking at the rooms like he suggested."

From room to room they traipsed, finding their way with the light from a book of matches that materialized from somebody's pocket and was struck one by one. The cover of the matchbook read, *Heartbreakers* (a local *gentleman's* club). But nobody mentioned it as they used the illumination the *sinful* matchbook provided.

When they got to the nursery, they saw the big, over-stuffed rocker that Mrs. Brenke, the nursery attendant, used every Sunday. She had been using it since some of the committee members had been in the nursery themselves.

"Oh, Mrs. Brenke," one crooned. "I can still feel her ample arms holding me and rocking me that time after I fell and skinned my knee. For a long time I thought the love of God was Mrs. Brenke's lap." Several others also shared their memories.

"Maybe Mrs. Brenke should be Church Member of the Year. How much do we pay her?" somebody proposed.

"She gets a check," Bankwell answered, "but she always signs it back to the church. We haven't bought toys for the nursery in...in years. Mrs. Brenke brings new ones—some she's made, some she's bought. I wonder how she does it on just a Social Security check."

They continued inching their way down the hall, huddling together, not wanting to stray much more than a step or two from the illumination of the match. They stopped abruptly when one burned out and another had to be lit.

The First Grade classroom had an inviting quality, even in the dark. Mrs. Jackson had been the first-grade teacher for decades. In fact, two committee members had learned from the gentle lady who told stories about Jesus just like she was seeing them through some video playing in her mind. Anybody who went to her class remembered the stories she told, and the way she got them across with crafts and mini-dramas. The curriculum couldn't have supplied all the ideas.

"Hey!" somebody exclaimed. "Maybe Mrs. Jackson should be Church Member of the Year. She's sure made an impact on the lives of the children who've been in her classes over the years."

Across the hall was the Junior High room where

Rusty Staples taught. The Senior High room was right next door, but it was empty. All the chairs had been moved into the Junior High room. Lying on a table was a blanket Rusty threw over her shoulder when she nursed her babies during the class. There'd been several of them over the years. Rusty was that special type of person who can relate to teenagers when they think all parents are stupid and don't understand at all.

"Whenever a girl gets pregnant, only the doctor knows before Rusty," someone said. "They trust her with all their secrets and problems. She started with the class in Junior High and not a one of them wanted to move up into the Senior High Class. They just stayed and included the new junior high kids as they came along. Even kids who went off to college come back to the class when they're home. They really need a bigger room. This one's so packed with chairs you can hardly move around. I'll bet there's not another church in town that can say they have teenagers hanging out the windows. These kids even get their parents to come, just so the kids can be with Rusty."

"I know! Let's nominate Rusty Staples as Church Member of the Year, for her contribution to the young people. She has a rare gift only a few people have and fewer are willing to share."

From room to room they went, inching along, having almost forgotten the mission they were on. In almost every room somebody had an idea of who their honoree should be.

Before long, they were back to the parlor where

they'd started from. It was still pitch black, but they could hear the noises of Jim Wire working. Then the lights began to come on in little fits and spurts. A fluorescent light that sat beneath a painting was the light they noticed first. The illuminated scene showed a mountainside with lots of folks sitting down. Then they could see the face of Jesus, seated, talking to the people. They could almost hear him saying,

> *...If one of you wants to be great, that person must be the servant of the rest;*
>
> *And if one of you wants to be first, that person must be the slave of all*
>
> Mark 10: 43–4 (TEV)

Little Boy's Easter

It was a bleak day—one of those where the weather is unsure if it's still winter or starting to be spring. For the last several minutes I had been watching a group of boys play football in the vacant lot across the street. One boy had a faint halting to his gait as he ran. Suddenly he stopped in mid-stride, reached down and rubbed his leg just behind the knee. I remembered another boy with a damaged leg, but I'll let him tell the story.

⌒

It was early when I woke up that day. Still dark, but the outside noises of trees and branches told me it would be light soon. The cowboys and Indians on my wallpaper were still asleep, so I couldn't talk to them. It seemed that daylight would never come.

I was going to my special new friend's house to

play. "Hurry up, sun. Come out and shine!" I said over and over again.

When my family finally woke up on that day I'd been waiting for, I rushed them, stirring the eggs and watching the toast. I had finished eating even before they'd buttered their toast. So I tried to go to special world. I go there when adults seem to be going in slow motion.

I couldn't find special world that morning. The arms of the clock seemed to be teasing me, moving backwards and forwards like loading trains do, blocking the tracks when you're already late for an important meeting.

Finally, my family was ready to go. Everybody piled into the 1953 Studebaker, fondly called The Gray Goose because of its pointy hood and wide-swept rear end. The narcissus patch was just starting to bloom as we wended our way down the long driveway.

There was Mom and Dad and me. And somebody else, too—my little sister, but she was still in Mom's tummy.

When we finally arrived, I was first out of the car, even though I'd been riding in the back seat. In my hurry to leave I forgot the sweater Mom had insisted I take—just in case.

The guys were playing movies. We had seen one on the kiddy show on Saturday. I was the German prisoner-of-war and there was this prison. It was in the outdoor patio with a barbecue pit. Tall, long, latticework brick walls rimmed each side of the pit.

It was one brick thick. They put me on a ledge as tall as my eyes. There were imaginary bars on the place, but they didn't say there were bars on top. I waited and waited for them to release me. Then I looked and saw they'd left me. My friend was playing football with some other guys. I wanted to go and play too, but I didn't want to break my holy vow not to go through the bars. Then I remembered they hadn't said anything about bars on the top. So, I climbed up hole by hole until I got to the top. I started to crawl over and that's the last thing I remember.

It was days later when I finally came to. There was a streak of white. I opened my eyes, wiped the thick, sleepy-seeds out and saw a nurse. Everything hurt. My right leg hurt most. But the ladies in white brought needles. Their sticks stung, but I didn't mind because they took the hurt away.

I was tied up in pulleys and weights. They called it "traction." It hurt when anyone jostled the bed. But the ladies in white always came with their magic needles. The needles would slip into my skin and make it better. Sometimes when the ladies in white took their time, I'd imagine the needle going in. That would help until the real needle came—the needle that sucked the fluid out of the vial labeled morphine. The needles were better than playing in the woods, until one day weeks later.

The old doctor came in, puffed on his cigar two times, dropping ashes down the front of his vest and told me, "No more shots! The morphine's got to stop!"

I had a bad dream that was so real. Black and pink spiders crawled around on the ceiling. I'm scared of spiders. They made webs that dangled down to my face and tickled my nose. But I couldn't brush them away, because my arms didn't work.

A yellow and purple python coiled on the frame of the traction, adding to the weight and making my leg feel like it might break off at the place where it was smashed. Coral snakes crawled out of my stomach and the Wicked Witch of the West wrote fire messages in the sky: "Die! Little boy—Die—No more needles! She cackled.

I felt like I was a hurt ocean. Nothing could stop the waves that rolled up and down my body, stopping—for so long—on that broken place.

After a long time, the waves went away. Then all that was left was the ticking clock I couldn't see. For days it ticked and ticked. Sometimes I thought it must have been ticking backwards. Ladies in white came and went. Mom and Dad came and went. Friends from church came and went. Most of the time I didn't look at them. They mustn't know about the spiders and snakes. They wouldn't believe me if I told them. Would you believe me, Mister?" I nodded my head in remembered agreement.

I tried to go to special world but I couldn't seem to get there. Then, one day after I stopped barfing in the silver pan, the spiders crawled back up their web ropes, the python slithered out the window. The coral snakes went crawling after it. And the Wicked Witch of the West turned to ashes.

Then the doctor came in; two men in white with him. Without a word, they unhooked the ropes and heavy stuff. I started crying because it hurt a lot. They slowly bent my leg. I didn't want to cry anymore, so I tried for special world again. And it came! I played like I was one of the birds flying in the a squiggledy vee outside the window in the sky. I looked down on the hospital and slowly floated until something else happened.

I looked back at my leg and it was kind of V-shaped—like the birds I'd been flying with. The men in white were wrapping my leg with some stuff that was all warm, wet, and white.

Then the doctor told me I'd be going home soon, maybe even by Easter. I was so happy. I couldn't wait to get home.

One morning Dad came in. Mom soon followed him. She was real big by now with my little sister inside her. A friend from church came in, too. Two men lifted me onto a stretcher. Then Mom dressed me in some new pj's and a bathrobe. And out they rolled me to the ambulance the church friend owned. I noticed the wind was much warmer than it was back on that awful day—much too warm for a just-in-case sweater.

I lifted up on my elbow. It seemed awfully quiet. There weren't cars on the streets where the stores were. Dad said there was a surprise for me and I couldn't wait to see what it was.

I was puzzled when I realized we weren't on the way home. That didn't seem right. Then I heard the church bells ringing. I realized it was Easter, and we were on our way to church.

I whispered the last memory verse I'd learned in Sunday School—I was glad when they said unto me, "Let us go into the house of the Lord" (Psalm 122: 1, KJV).

Gently, Mr. Johnson and Dad lifted me out of the ambulance. They made a chair for me with their arms and started up the 30 steps to church. I know there are 30 because I count them each Sunday.

The leaves were back on the trees and pansies were blooming. Even with the door closed I could hear everybody singing. "Jesus Christ is Risen Today," I sang as loud as I could. I could smell the lilies and candles everywhere.

They carried me in and headed for our place—the third pew from the front on the right side. As they carried me in, people stopped singing and started clapping. I cried.

The minister read something from the Psalms.

⤺

The young boy didn't have to tell me what passage the minister read him and the worshippers on that special Easter. It would have been Psalm 30:5—*"Weeping may endure for a night, but joy cometh in the morning"* (KJV).

I know because—you see—the little boy—is me!

The Day Of The Lord Is Coming!

It was an awful night! I was sick in body and spirit. I tossed and turned, trying to find the magic spot. About the time I'd nod off to sleep, a coughing fit would strike and I'd have to sit upright in bed to keep from choking on the collection of mess I was bringing up from the bowels of my lungs. I'd taken some cough medicine—the sure-fire stuff that was supposed to arrest any cough. Dope was the alleged magic ingredient. But nothing seemed to stop the cycle. And it seemed as though I'd never rest. I felt awful! And a terrible sadness had a stranglehold on my very soul.

I glanced over at the clock for the umpteenth time. All that greeted me was a winking light and the message that little more than a few minutes had passed since the last time I'd looked when it was four in the morning. I decided to try to read myself sleepy. I built a nest with the pillows and propped myself up to read, but the book was on the dresser and not on the nightstand where it was supposed to be. I couldn't remember moving it—I never moved it! But some supernatural force had levitated it to a place where I was forced to get out of bed to fetch it. I got up on my elbows in preparation Then a catch in my side—one from too much deep-lung coughing—caused me to wince as I assumed a sitting position. But I retrieved the book, got the pillows all fluffed and arranged for reading, and returned to the place of my frustration. I nestled down in the mound of pillows, picked up the book, settled in—and the catch in my side reintroduced itself. It must be a muscle I'd pulled. I moved to another position I thought would ease it. It didn't. So I tried even another position—one I was sure would provide relief. It didn't. I tried a series of new ways to arrange the pillows and/or myself, but it would pinch me no matter how I scrunched around to get comfortable. Reading didn't work!

I snapped off the light to explore other options. I thought I might be able to contort myself into a half-lying down and half-sitting up position. Logic told me I'd be upright enough to avoid the coughing, but still prone enough to find comfort and the sweet oblivion of sleep. A new eruption from the depths got me coughing again. And the paroxysm made the pulled muscle even more aggravated.

I glanced around the room, looking at the familiar detail of things and furniture and clutter I called my inner sanctum. I noticed there was a faint glimmer peeking through the curtains. It was starting to get light. Even though I couldn't sleep, I still didn't want to wake up either. Banging the mattress in frustration, I tried to block out the demon dawn by pulling the covers over my head. I thought that the cocoon of darkness might bring on sleep. But that made me feel smothered, so I pushed my head out of the prison of covers and a little beam of light wended its way toward my eyes. I moved over a bit and the beam seemed to be following me. I looked up at it and saw the offending infant sunbeam was sneaking into my world through a small gap in the curtains. In reality, the beam of light was pursuing me because my wandering through the wasteland of the sheets paralleled the path the light was taking as the sun began its trek through the heavens.

For a moment, I just lay there with the beam of light boring into my forehead. It strangely warmed me. Its comforting presence seemed to burrow right into my skull and spread throughout my body to every aching part. The muscles that brought on the coughing relaxed. The knots in my back that felt like I was being stuck by a hot poker eased. The tension of mind and body began to fade away. Even some of the pain of the soul began to go away.

About that time the cat jumped up on the bed and lay gently down on my shoulder. It commenced a brmm, brmm of purring right in my ear. I was able to close my eyes in peace for the first time that night—or should I say that night and morning. In my mind's eye

I gazed up at the gentle, warm beam of light which brought a healing presence to every part of me and sensed that rest was near at hand.

That's the last thing I remembered before sleep finally came—hours of luxurious, restful, body and soul healing sleep. When I finally roused myself, I was a totally different human being from the one who'd wrestled with the night. I felt calm, my coughing more manageable, my muscles relaxed. And I was able to sit up and look the day straight in the eye anxious to see what the world had in store for me.

But for you who obey me, my saving power will rise on you like the sun's rays. You will be as free and happy as calves let out of a stall.

Malachi 4:2 (TEV)

Sir, We Would See Jesus

The church in Vernon, Texas, where my Father grew up has something that catches a preacher's attention. The sanctuary is rather spartan: there's little artifice, ornament, or decoration. There is just a cross on a communion table, a table with plain lines that is sturdy, but has nothing that would draw one's attention to it otherwise. The cross is brass with no curlicues or fancy etching, just the plain metal crosspieces. But towering over all these is the pulpit. It's big, even for the size of the sanctuary. It stands firmly rooted in the center of the altar area. It too has no carvings, just straight lines that seem to move one's eyes heavenward. There is one ornamentation that few might see and no one would see unless cleaning or mounting the steps to perform the intended function. Gracing the center of the pulpit's dais—just below the place where a preacher would place sermon notes or manuscript—is a piece of marble that has been ornately and delicately carved. It reads, "*Sir, we would see Jesus.*" That's quite a set-up for a preacher about to speak. It's intimidating, but also challenging. It reminds preachers what they're really supposed to be about.

Of course, the quote comes from John's gospel. What might the scene where these words were spoken have looked like back then?

∽

It was a holiday madhouse. People jostling and pushing, moving around. Today we might say it's like getting around New Orleans during Mardi Gras. And that's not a bad description because there was a feast being celebrated—a religious feast—Passover. Just like New Orleans and Mardi Gras, people have come from far and near to celebrate this religious festival in Jerusalem. And not all of them are Jews—the people of the religious festival. John tells us there were people of all sorts of different kinds there, including a small group of Greeks.

The Greeks slowly press up the long, steep set of steps. Step by step they progress, getting pushed and jostled by the crowds going the same place they're going. They reach a huge gateway. They walk through. The scene that greets them is pandemonium. There are souvenir stands. Places where people can change money, since only special coins can be given as gifts to the God who began the festival. There are people hawking their wares, too. One shoves something in their faces and calls out, "Prime pigeons, just perfect for sacrifice. There's not a blemish to be found on any of these. Just right for your special offering!"

Another touts, "Lambs! Sacrificial lambs for sale. They've been inspected by the priests and certified perfect for sacrifice. With their dying bleat your prayers will be lifted up to the One True God."

Within just a few steps the merchants and people become a blur of sound and motion, color and spectacle. The Greeks are in the Court of the Gentiles, the furthermost into the Jewish Temple most folks could go. Along with the merchants selling their wares, there's a babble of languages from every corner of the earth. All here for one thing: to celebrate the salvation of the Hebrews from slavery in Egypt. Later on there would be special ceremonial feasts, and all manner of other celebrations. But, for now, the Greeks are with the polyglot of folks crowding this place where Jew and non-Jew alike meet on the Temple Mount.

The Greeks are moving from one clot of people to another. There are various rabbis and other teachers talking to a huddle of followers and interested bystanders. From group to group they move, their progress slowed by the crowds. They go from one group of rabbi and followers to another, touching one person on the shoulder and inquiring about something, then moving on. Sometimes the person queried looks them up and down, noticing their clothes. A group or two is annoyed because they've been interrupted. Another group pulls back like they've been scalded when they realize the people asking them questions are Greeks.

A man named Philip notices them moving from one group to another. The group, whose clothes identify them as Greeks, approach him, "Sir, we want to see Jesus," the leader of the Greeks says and the others nod their heads enthusiastically and hopefully. Philip goes over to another guy named Andrew. Together they approach their rabbi, their teacher. Then they go back and bring the Greeks over. The rabbi smiles warmly at them and speaks. His speech is unusual for Jerusalem: it has the broad accents of Galilee, but nobody seems to mind.

Where would Christians of today take folks to see Jesus? When asked the same question the Greeks asked, where would followers take them? Join me in a journey of the heart.

_ᴒ_

The classroom is an attractive one. All the walls are covered with pictures and quotes from Scripture written in flowing calligraphy. There are plants growing. Each Sunday there is the kind of happy noise that occurs when children are learning with gusto. At the center of the Sunday hubbub would be Eve. She's one of those special people whom kids love and flock to. She has that unique gift of being a child and entering into a child's world, yet still being the adult. The classroom is the one marked *Junior High* on the door. Eve's the only person in the history of that congregation who actually volunteers to teach the Junior Highs. Though they've never been told that, the kids somehow know it and pour out of the woodwork every Sunday morning. Sometimes even parents are dragged along to church by the children, jubilantly hungry to learn about their faith.

One frazzled mother proclaimed for all the parents, "Johnny actually gets *us* up on Sunday mornings so he can be sure he gets to Sunday School to be with Eve. A while back a houseguest asked my husband and me a question about the Bible. We looked at each other, clueless. But Johnny answered their question without missing a beat."

"Eve taught us about that," he proudly announced.

This Sunday there's a huddle of kids waiting around the door for Eve to arrive. They wonder what she's going to do with the sheets of newsprint she's carrying with her.

Now, in the creative chaos, Eve is laying out sheets of newsprint in the midst of noisy questions about what they're going to do. With an excited smile she declares,

"We're going to make a Bible newspaper today. But first we need to decide its name. It comes from Jerusalem from Jesus' time.

One hand pops up, "We could call it the Holy City Herald!" Another almost shouts, "Or the Jerusalem Journal," and before you know it, the kids are jumping feet first into the project, getting their things together.

As latecomers arrive, they're quickly included. The level of happy noise is almost deafening. But nobody seems to care.

"Let's see," Eve says, "Joanna, you do the fashion news. Here're some passages from the Bible about a woman named Lydia who dyed cloth. And here's a book with some pictures of what clothes looked like back then. Read the passages and look at the pictures. Then draw some fashion ads that might have been back then. And write a story about a fashion show. Get some other kids to work with you."

A knot of children gets eagerly to their task.

"Oh, I almost forgot! Here's a story Jesus told about the lilies of the field."

Other kids are jumping excitedly, waiting for their assignments. "Jack," Eve continues, "you do the sports page. Oh, you could write something about chariot races and chess matches. They used to play a game that was kind of like chess. In fact just before Jesus was crucified, some soldiers played it, using Jesus as one of the game pieces.

"Jeremy, you have the editorial page. Write about the importance of Passover and celebrating religious feasts and festivals. You know, when Jesus began the Lord's Supper he and the disciples were celebrating Passover.

"And Rosemary—ah—you could write about the 300th annual Esther beauty pageant and make up some winners.

"And the food section—who wants to make up

some recipes about loaves and fishes?" An eager hand shoots up and the food section begins to take shape.

"And who wants to do the want ads?" Another hand shoots up and a small flurry of activity commences.

The Sunday School superintendent sticks his head in the door. He shakes his head slowly back and forth in amazement. He wants to mention to Eve that it would be better if she stuck closer to the curriculum provided for her. But it's obvious he wouldn't be heard. And maybe it would be a futile request because he'd asked it before, and got vague answers from her. And this chaos still took place in spite of his efforts to get things calmed down and more focused on what the children normally would be studying.

He'd said just this sort of thing at a Christian Education Committee meeting and almost got his head chopped off because they thought Eve was doing a great job—"Wish we had more like her," one committee member bluntly stated. So he backed off. Maybe it was a losing cause—after all, they were learning the Bible, even if in a somewhat unorthodox fashion.

Slowly the newspaper mock-up begins to take shape. When it's finished, Eve holds up each page. "Here's what it looks like. You all did great work. Wow! We'll have to get a copy of this printed in the church newsletter and put on the Sunday School bulletin board."

Now the church copier is needed. Slowly the paper gets reproduced for each child, specially printed and individually marked with each child's name.

The proud smiles of accomplishment beam on each face. Not one paper is rolled up and stuffed away to be forgotten after church. As parents are located by each bubbling child, the newspaper is proudly produced and described in detail, pointing to the section that child worked on. And upon reaching home most of the newspapers are proudly placed on the front of the refrigerator, fastened with a magnet, or tacked up on a special place in each child's room.

Eve, we want to see Jesus.

❧

Jack pulls into the driveway of the house where his friend Bill lives. He gets out of the car, picks up the newspaper, goes to the mailbox, gets the mail and, using a key, lets himself in through the kitchen door. The kitchen has a musty smell, like it had been closed up while the occupant went away on vacation. There's a fine layer of dust everywhere, but it's relatively straight. All the dishes and food are in their place and put away.

Jack locates a dust rag and begins to hit the counter area where he's going to prepare food. He dampens a cloth with some cleanser and wipes the counter area again. Realizing this would be a task requiring more work than he could afford the time to do, he locates the *to-do* list tacked by a magnet to the refrigerator and scribbles instruction for the maid who comes in once a week.

Then he reaches into the pantry for a box of oatmeal, after he's puts water in a teakettle and sets it to boil. He fixes a tray with a fresh daisy out of his garden in a small vase and sets it on a low cabinet. Then pours a big scoop of oatmeal into a bowl, shakes in some cinnamon and some raisins, and adds a generous scoop of a protein supplement and sets the microwave to cooking it. When it's finished, he adds a heaping scoop of brown sugar and stirs the fragrant mixture until it's dissolved.

By now the kettle is whistling merrily. He pours the hot water into a cheery teapot he's brought with him that contains a measure of herbal tea, which bursts out with a fragrant odor as the water is poured on it. Taking a tray from the cabinet, he places the mouth-watering preparations on top of a doily he's arranged on the tray. Jack picks up the delectable offering and heads into the dining room.

"Bill," he calls out, "I'm here."

As he walks through the dining room and living room, he makes mental notes of things the maid will need to do. But there's one thing he can do now. He puts the food down and opens up every window he can reach and the front door to let the fresh spring air enter the closed up, tomb-like house. He picks the food tray up again, and then walks toward the hall and the only room that's lived in. It's dark. So he lifts up the shades, opens the windows to air out the stench that has permeated the room during the night.

It's only then that Bill can be seen—and what can

be seen is more like being hinted at because there's not much left of him to be seen. His body barely makes a ripple in the tangle of bedclothes. Bill's covered with sores. Deep coughs choke from his throat as his chest heaves and heaves to breathe.

"The pneumonia's bad today, isn't it, Bill?" Jack says sympathetically. A nod answers him as Jack puts on latex gloves and busies himself. He helps Bill to sit in a nearby chair and begins pulling off the musty sheets and blanket. He wads up the mountain of tissues and stuff that have gathered around the bed and throws them away. Next the bedpan and portable urinal are taken to the bathroom, emptied, rinsed out, sprayed with a fresh disinfectant and returned to their place.

Only then does Jack place the tray on Bill's lap. The aroma of the fragrant food by this time has wafted throughout the room. Spoonful by slow spoonful Bill eats while Jack fetches fresh sheets and starts to remake the bed. All the pillows are fluffed into crisp pillowcases, and the dirty linen is whisked away.

His tasks accomplished, Jack sits down and puts a gloved hand on Bill's arm. They talk about small things—how the Astros are looking for this year, the basketball playoffs, and some current events. Bill's face begins to gain a little animation as the food and freshness of the room suffuse him. After most of the oatmeal and some of the tea has been finished, Jack helps Bill back into the bed, pulling fresh sheets over the remainder of what once had been a robust, healthy man. Then he goes back to the kitchen, fetches a pitcher of ice and pours the remainder of the tea on it. He leaves it by Bill's bedside along with a colorful glass he's brought from home.

They chat some more. Jack helps with the mountain of pills that have to be swallowed individually and with difficulty. He stands and looks at his watch. Jack's already late for work, but he doesn't rush his departure.

"Well, got to put my nose to the ole grindstone. Sherry and the kids send their love. See you tomorrow!" He closes the windows and doors, then leaves.

As Jack returns through the house he remembers the commemorative quilt that's been traveling from town to town. It will be in their city next week. He closes the windows and doors, making sure they're locked. "They'll be putting Bill's name on the traveling quilt soon." He shakes his head in sorrow, and lets himself out.

Jack, we want to see Jesus!

John's gospel tells us, "Some Greeks were among those who'd gone to Jerusalem to worship during the Passover festival. They went to Philip and said, "Sir, we want to see Jesus."

Philip went and told Andrew and the two of them went and told Jesus."

John 12:20 (TEV)

She Hath Borne Our Griefs

Tucked away in a high meadow on the border between France and Spain lies a small village. In the 1930s it was rarely touched by the outside world, except for the lumbering bus that creaked into town twice a week. A smuggler or two took advantage of the hundreds of caves which pocked the mountains and the web of goat-like trails that eventually wended their way into Spain.

That's the way the village was when Marie Duvalier returned after attending the university in Bordeaux. As far back as anyone in the village could remember, no one—much less a girl—had gone off to the university. And few had traveled to Bordeaux. The nun who taught the children the basic skills needed to be a shopkeeper or a farmer had recognized that Marie was unique. By the time she'd been in school five years, she had exhausted the meager supply of books the village possessed and had read many of them five or six times.

The nun vowed that this child must go outside the village to fully develop her mind and quench her thirst for knowledge. So she badgered the parish priest to speak to the bishop. "Sister," he finally said, "You're like the importunate widow Jesus spoke of who kept on pestering the judge for justice until he finally gave in. I'll write the bishop this afternoon and get the letter on the bus for Bordeaux."

"Do you want me to write the letter for you, Father?" the nun offered.

He smiled at her persistence. "No, Sister, I believe I can do that on my own. I can make a convincing case on Marie's behalf. She'll get that invitation to the convent school you want for her."

The headmistress of the convent school was a former classmate, so the nun wrote to her, too: "Sister, please look out for Marie. Take her as far as she can go. I hold her dear to my heart."

Marie was accepted, but the convent school hadn't been able to contain her either. She breezed through every course offered and yearned for a larger library. Again the village priest was asked to intercede with the bishop. By this time the bishop had met Marie and was as impressed with her abilities as the others had been. He set up a college education for her paid for by the diocese.

On holidays Marie could usually scrape together enough money to take the lumbering bus to her home in the mountains. Most times the entire town knew she was coming and many would be waiting to greet her. These were festive gatherings for the village folk. The visits often coincided with special religious festivals, so they acquired the kind of reverence and joy normally reserved for special saints of the church.

After a few years, cholera scythed its way through the mountain village. And one of the ones cut down was the beloved nun who taught the school. Word was sent to the diocese that another teacher was needed. Marie was working in the bishop's office when the word arrived. She ran to her quarters and packed her belongings. She soon stood in the bishop's reception room, bags in hand with a bedraggled straw hat jauntily angled on her head. She handed the letter from her village to the bishop and, even before he could read the opening sentences, announced: "I'm going back to teach the children." Her voice had a firmness the bishop knew would brook no interference.

"But, Marie, my dear, you only have a few months before graduation."

She didn't utter a word. The jut of her jaw conveyed her determination. And so it was that she stepped onto the bus bound for home to teach as she herself had once been taught. One village after another slowed progress. Marie couldn't stay seated and got off at each stop, pacing back and forth, urging passengers and baggage along. Finally, her village was in sight. She saw the craggy face of the mountain she loved, the one she'd decided looked like the face of a cow.

Only a scattering of people saw her step down from the bus, but the word spread like wildfire. A happy villager offered her a ride home in his wagon. She threw her bags and parcels on the bed of the wagon, and even before they had gotten to the edge of town, a crowd thronged to greet her. The driver stopped. They all wondered why Marie was coming home just now. Some asked if she knew Sister had died. A tear welled in the corner of her eye as she acknowledged the sad news.

"Who's going to teach the children now that she's gone?" many asked.

"I've come to teach them myself," she announced.

The villagers buzzed with questions: "But you're not a sister, are you? No one's taught the children except nuns." Marie nodded and the wagon got underway.

By the time she'd reached her family farm, Marie's mother was waiting for her, She frantically brushed flour off her hands with her apron, but didn't notice the swath of white across her forehead that a stray hand had left in haste.

So, Marie became the village teacher. The students rejoiced that school had taken a different shape. Instead of being in the squat, stone building, the classroom ranged around the village and sometimes deep into the mountains. Rudimentary science was learned on a mountain path or by watching cows in a field. Reading and numbers had a towering mountain for a backdrop.

Years passed. The villagers wondered when a nun would come so Marie could return to school herself. Only her mother and the parish priest knew the truth:

Marie had written the bishop that she wanted to continue with the children.

After a time, faint lines traced by the sun finely etched Marie's face. But her beauty wasn't diminished. Her gray-green eyes maintained their lively inquisitiveness. Her lush auburn hair continued to flounce down her back in loose curls. And her shapely athletic body grew even firmer and fuller as she led children through the mountains, teaching as they went.

Occasionally an awkward farm boy would come calling, hat clenched nervously in hand, feet shuffling in circles. She greeted each warmly, but none came more than two or three times. It was as if they were afraid of her—or felt they might not rise to her expectations.

And so it remained until the war reached out to touch the village. An almost invisible stream of refugees seeped into town during the night, then seeped out again, led along their way to places the village folk knew, but wouldn't tell the booted, helmeted strangers who came searching. If you looked closely at the coats of the quiet pilgrims passing through, you could see where the fabric was darker in one patch. The patch where the yellow Star of David had been sewn.

For Marie, the children were the saddest. Many had been yanked out of boarding schools and were separated from or had no parents because of the thoroughness of the German soldiers and their French minions.

Marie mixed the fleeing children in among her own. Even looking closely it was hard to pick them out from the others as they bounced through the fields and paths, eagerly learning as they went. Their tell-tale garments had been replaced by ones garnered from village children. The only clue to their difference came from the glazed-over look of emptiness that etched their faces into premature maturity. They had suffered so much, they were beyond tears.

In search of the refugees, squads of soldiers would descend unannounced amid clouds of dust. Sometimes they would scoop up a batch of Jewish refugees and sometimes not. Those who managed to escape were spirited by secret groups of villagers along torturous goat paths across the ridge into Spain.

Marie was one of the busiest of the villagers. The soldiers were used to her wandering around with her gaggle of students in tow. So it was simple to add three or four more and escort them to a cave hidden by a cascading waterfall. Other villagers would take them on to a spot in Spain where they could be reunited with family members—if any were alive.

An unvoiced defiance was sensed throughout the village. No one divulged the hiding place. The parish priest had taught them the Jews were God's chosen and anyone in need was their brother.

For years people in the village snickered when they spoke of the great hiding place the haystack behind police headquarters had made.

Soon, however, the pressure began to mount. No matter how diligent the soldiers were, their haul of Jews was dwindling. The district head of the Gestapo was particularly under fire because the quota of Jews sent east to the camps wasn't being met—not even close. He summoned the agent in charge of Marie's village to headquarters in Biarritz. Even the promised pleasures of that seaside resort couldn't assuage the fear that knotted in the pit of the agent's stomach.

"You're not doing your duty to the Fatherland," the district chief shrieked. "Because of your laziness, I'm about to be summoned to Paris. I'm facing a one-way ticket to the Eastern Front."

The agent was sweating profusely in spite of the bone-chilling cold. "I don't know why we can't find the Jews. We're working double shifts. Everyone is exhausted from the efforts. Maybe a few extra patrols might help."

"Extra patrols! I have none to spare! Do you expect me to shut down the work someplace else where the results are more promising? Redouble your efforts. As of now, unless you meet the quotas and make up the shortages already incurred, you'll be reduced in rank. And if that doesn't motivate you, you might find yourself on one of those trains going East."

When the agent returned to the village, his superior's rage was passed down the chain of command until even the lowest of soldiers was on heightened alert. The sounds of their motorcycles could be heard night and day. But the harder they worked, the fewer Jews found! After the first month of total commitment, the number of refugees with the missing yellow star patches had trickled to almost nothing.

The frustrating, unrewarding work drew longer hours and daily brow-beatings from the village chief. Tempers were short; villagers were beaten for no apparent reason. They began to close themselves up in their homes, venturing out only in large groups. Young women stayed at home unless they were in the company of the village priest or in a large group.

What made the life even more frustrating was that no female would *accommodate* the soldiers. Even the one prostitute in the town refused her services in spite of the wads of German marks offered. They ached for female companionship. Wherever the good-looking school teacher went, lust-filled eyes followed her. Each German tried to corner her alone. But they could never catch her without a group of children with her. She became a fixation to these young men who were far from home with an odious task and feeling hate wherever they turned.

One day a patrol stumbled on a young girl on the brink of womanhood. She was searching for a lost lamb. The soldiers circled her, grinning from ear to ear and ogling her budding body from every angle. One cad reached out and snatched her shawl off her shoulders. She screamed. Another tore at her blouse. A third grabbed at her skirt so hard she stumbled to the ground. A patrol leader slowly began unbuttoning his tunic. Then unbuckled his holster and belt. He was unzipping his pants when the girl cried, "I'll do anything you want only don't do *that* to me." She began sobbing and choking, every limb shivering in fear.

"There's one possible solution," the soldier said.

"Tell me about the Jewish children. Where are they hiding? I know they're around. Tell us where they are and we'll let you go."

"The teacher has them."

"How is that possible?"

"She puts them in with the other students and takes them to the mountains and hides them. I swear I don't know where, but probably in one of the caves near the border."

The words were hardly out of her mouth before one of the soldiers disrobed, followed by another and another—and lastly—the leader. During the ravaging violence the girl choked on her vomit and died.

"Imagine that—hiding in plain sight—right under our noses," the village Gestapo agent mused. "How clever! Well, that will end soon!"

The next day the young girl's abused, broken body was discovered by shepherds. Gravely they carried her into the village to the church. Somber-faced old women ministered to her, preparing her for the funeral mass. The tension exuded from every villager's pores. But the Germans had smug looks on their faces and didn't seem to mind the palpable hatred directed their way.

The afternoon following the funeral, a group of students wended its way toward the cave. Marie pointed out this tree or that bird, then sat them down by a brook to talk about the death of their friend. She brooded over how much to tell them, finally deciding the whole truth was best. They recited a rosary together and the sextet of Jewish children joined in

with, "Hear, O Israel, the Lord–and the Lord alone—
is our God" (Deuteronomy 6:4).

When they arrived at the waterfall, Marie talked
about where the water came from and where it went,
reminding them of the brook where they had mourned
together. They were abuzz with comments. Then she
hustled them under the waterfall into the cave. They
all thought this was great fun. A couple of the boys
went back and forth under the cascade until they were
totally soaked. She was about to herd the last one in
when she heard the roar of motorcycle engines.

In the distance she saw the cloud of dust kicked up
by the racing machines. She looked at the students—
and the Jewish children. What she had feared was happening! A young girl felt her teacher's fear and began
to cry. Like an epidemic the others joined her. Marie's
mind raced, even faster than her heart was beating. She
wondered what to do with the village children. They
should be safe, but she feared they'd be lumped in with
the Jewish children. Then a calm came over her.

She led all the children deep into the cave, deeper
than she'd ever gone before. She decided her students
would be safer in hiding with the refugees than wit-
nessing what was about to happen. Pairing one older
child with a younger one, she hid them in places it
would be difficult to discover even with full daylight.

"Don't come out," she told them. "Don't move if
someone comes into the cave. Don't utter a sound—
no matter what you hear. No—matter—what—you—
hear! Let no one know you're here until the man

with the shepherd's crook comes. Only then may you speak." She made each one swear a solemn oath, then she headed for the mouth of the cave.

She walked through the waterfall, took a shuddering breath, and started to unbutton her shirt, then her skirt. Shaking with fear, she stepped out of her shoes. Her eyes glanced once in the direction of the approaching dust cloud. Then she neatly folded her garments and arranged them carefully by a nearby rock.

She stepped into the cascading water that hid the mouth of the cave. Her breath came in quick gasps from the shock of the icy water. She began running her hands over her naked body as if she were bathing.

The cloud of dust grew. The roar of engines crescendoed. A hail of stones and screeching tires announced the soldiers' arrival. Marie screamed and acted surprised. Covering herself as best as she could with her hands, she tried to reach for her clothing.

One by one, each man got off his motorcycle and brushed the dust off his pants and boots. Sounds of metallic raspings and clicking buttons made their intentions quite plain. Marie looked up at the sky and squeezed her eyes shut. The last thing she saw was a vulture circling overhead.

Some hours later the shepherd with the crook came, as planned, to fetch the children. His wife was with him. She was to accompany Marie and the village children home while he was to bring the Jewish children on to the next stop. They found her bloody, bruised, ravaged body crumpled in a heap on top of a flat horizontal rock. Her eyes were still squeezed shut; her body, cold.

As they entered the cave, frightened cries greeted them. Slowly each pair came out from their hiding place. They told of the screams they'd heard—and the laughs. "A soldier peeked into the cave one time," a young boy offered, " but he didn't come in very far."

According to the prophet Isaiah, "The Lord says, 'My servant will succeed in his task; he will be highly honored. Many people were shocked when they saw him; he was so disfigured that he hardly looked human. But now many nations will marvel at him, and kings will be speechless with amazement. They will see and understand something they had never known.'

"The people replied: 'Who would have believed what we now report?...We despised him and rejected him; he endured suffering and pain...endured the suffering that should have been ours, the pain that we should have borne...Because of our sin he was wounded, beaten because of the evil we did. We are healed by the punishment he suffered, made whole by the blows he received...He was treated harshly, but endured it humbly, he never said a word. Like a lamb about to be slaughtered, he never said a word. He was arrested and sentenced and led off to die, and no one cared about his fate. He was put to death for the sin of our people... even though he'd never committed a crime.'

"Surely he hath borne our griefs and carried our sorrows."

Selections from Isaiah 52 and 53 (TEV & KJV)

Sin: People's Drug Of Choice

You should have seen Jake Miller when he stepped out of the doors of the hospital. He opened up his arms to drink in the sun. Before he knew it, his fists clenched and you could hear him shout, "*Yes!*" When we think of somebody leaving the hospital, we normally think of wheelchairs and people who don't think they need them—but it's hospital policy. Well, this wasn't that kind of hospital. It was one of those hospitals: the kind the scandal magazines revel in when *stars* have to go there. Some call them sanitariums—that was the old name; or drying out places—that's the cruder term present people might use. You see, Jake Miller is an alcoholic. Alcohol had had him by the throat for so long he couldn't remember when Jack wasn't his best friend. "You know, Jack Daniels," he used to say when friends even looked like they wanted to talk to him about his drinking.

And now he was out—sprung—dried out—and he was so elated he almost floated to his car that he was allowed to drive home, back and forth to work and nowhere else. His license had been suspended, but he'd managed to wheedle a hardship permit since there was no one else to take him to work. You see, his wife and children left long ago. He'd managed to hold onto his job, though—or rather the company had put up with him—maybe because they were being nice, or maybe because he was the best at what he did—at least when he was sober, which he mostly was when he went to work. But he was out! Out of the hospital!

He opened the door to his car and the fumes nearly knocked him over. A bottle of *Jack* had tipped over—or been tipped over—on the passenger seat. He waved the door back and forth in mock airing out and reached over for his former friend, Jack, the half-empty bottle from which the sickening/inviting vapors wafted. He looked *Jack* right in the eye, hesitated a brief moment and took great pleasure heaving ole *Jack* as far as he could out into the woods surrounding the hospital. He listened for the sound that used to make him cringe in disappointment and heard it: the clatter of breaking glass. He couldn't help doing some skips and jumps. Then into his car he went and drove back into the world.

About a week or so later he was out with some of his buddies. They'd gone to the local watering hole after work. All the way to their favorite joint they quizzed Jake about where he'd been. He fobbed off one query after another with vague answers and attempts to distract them onto other topics.

Inside they each went to the bar and ordered. Jack hesitated a moment or so until he could be out of earshot when he ordered. "Perrier with a twist," he told the bartender who looked askance, but filled the order with a shrug of his shoulders.

At their usual table there were an assortments of drinks—a glass of wine, a beer, something in a glass tinkling with ice and one of those pink drinks. You know, the ones that come with the little umbrellas stuck in them. And, of course, there was, firmly implanted in front of Jake—Perrier with a twist. *At least it looks like a drink,* Jake told himself. His friends noticed the change in color from his usual libation. After one smell they knew it was Perrier, but they all teased him asking to smell it just to make sure.

Finally, Will screwed up his courage. "Jake, are you on the wagon?"

"Yes," Jake muttered under his breath. He tried to steer the conversation into other areas, but to no avail. "I've been on medical leave at a hospital to get off the booze," he admitted sheepishly.

"Jake, how much did that hospital help you, you've been eating antacids like candy ever since we got in here. Maybe you need to take ole St. Paul's advice—a little wine for the stomach." That drew a chuckle from all the guys. And Jake, fleetingly, but longingly, ogled the array of spirits on display. Pointing to the wine rack, he quipped lamely, "Perrier's a lot cheaper." And throughout the evening Perrier it continued to be.

Sometime later that week, the company president called the staff working on the Lamberson contract into the executive suite. "We've just got the Lamberson contract signed," he exulted. "It's time for a celebration. Let's pop the cork on that bottle of Dom Perignon I've been saving for a special occasion. With this contract signed and sealed, we're floating in higher cotton than we ever have before."

The president made a presentation of uncorking the bottle, pointed the initial spewing into his mouth, then with a flourish, started pouring out a glass of champagne for each of the people who'd been working 70-hour weeks on this project. Jake had been picked up for DWI after the celebration when the team had finally completed the Lamberson proposal. Now they could all relax and enjoy the success of their efforts. But, when the president began to pour a glass for Jake, he stammered, "I can't anymore." He passed his glass of bubbly to the next person in line.

It looked odd that Jake's hand wasn't raised for the toast like everybody else's. He felt left out. He'd worked hard to get where he was—in fact, the stress had been the cause of much of his drinking. Out of the corner of his eye, Jake noticed the boss eyeing him. In a moment of fantasy, he saw the man's face twist up into a serious grin and heard him say, "You'd better drink with us if you want to be one of the movers and shakers." Jake shook his head to rid himself of the image. He exited the party as soon as he gracefully could.

He waited for a friend who'd agreed to drop him off at an AA meeting. They arrived early and had some time to kill. "Jake," the friend pondered, "just how much good did that hospital do you—and how much do these meetings help? Could you pour yourself one drink and stop? I just wondered if you could. Stands to rights that if you were cured you could. Just one—and go on as if nothing had happened. That seems to be the ultimate test of your recovery."

The friend popped a beer open and offered one to Jake who had to resist the automatic reaction to accept the camaraderie of the brew. The high of the hospital was miles away.

> Jesus returned from the Jordan full of the Holy Spirit and was led by the Spirit into the desert, where he was tempted by the Devil for forty days. In all that time he ate nothing, so that he was hungry when it was over.
>
> The Devil said to him, "If you're God's Son, order this stone to turn into bread."
>
> But Jesus answered, "The scripture says, 'people cannot live on bread alone.' "
>
> Then the Devil took him up and showed him in a second all the kingdoms of the world. "I'll give you all this power and all this wealth," the Devil told him, "It has all been handed over to me, and I can

give it to anyone I choose. All this will be yours, then, if you worship me."

Jesus answered, "the scripture says, ' Worship the Lord your God and serve only God!'"

Then the devil took him to Jerusalem and set him on the highest point of the Temple, and said to him, "If you're God's Son, throw yourself down from here. For the scripture says, ' God will order his angels to take good care of you.' It also says ' They will hold you up with their hands so that not even your feet will be hurt on the stones.'"

But Jesus answered, "The scripture says, ' Do not put the Lord your God to the test.'"

When the Devil finished tempting Jesus in every way, he left him for a while.

Luke 4:1–13 (TEV)

I Am The Vine

I guess I must have been six or seven. Company was coming over for supper. People were coming over I really liked—people who didn't brush me aside as being *just a kid*. Mom had been giving the house a real going over. There'd been vacuuming, dusting, arranging stuff, straightening paintings that had mysteriously become slightly askew. In short, the house was getting ready for our special friends to come over for supper. Mom had planned a scrumptious dinner. I'd gone to the grocery store with her to buy all the food. There were plump, crisp bell peppers, fresh, firm tomatoes, a big red onion, fresh garlic and chicken. For Mom's *stinky salad*—that's what we called it—there was crisp green, leafy lettuce, more tomatoes, mushrooms, sharp cheddar cheese. I could almost taste the delectable food that awaited us. My stomach growled just thinking about it. I'd been able to do a few things to help

203

Mom, but she wanted to do most things by herself to see that they got done just like she wanted them.

But I wanted to do something special on my own. Something that would tell these people just how much I liked them paying attention to me, talking to me, asking my thoughts and opinions. Most folks just ruffled my hair (I didn't like that at all) and acted like I wasn't there. I wanted to do something special. And then the perfect thing came to me.

I took my little ladder and the garden shears and headed out into the woods where I knew there was something that would make things special. It was hard dragging that ladder through the woods. There were brambles and tangles. Leaves and pine straw matted the ground like a marshmallow carpet. But I forged on, knowing just where it was that I could find that thing that would make the occasion extra special. I walked and walked, struggling with the ladder and all.

Slowly I knew that I was getting close. I couldn't see it, but I knew it was there because I smelled it. The scent got stronger and sweeter until I finally saw it. A tree covered with vines—vines you could smell from yards away. The vine has several East Texas folk names—like wild jasmine, yellow jasmine. Since then I've heard it called Carolina jasmine. It has a yellow, trumpet-like flower that has a wondrous fragrance when it's blooming. As a child I thought the fragrance was a cross between honeysuckle and gardenias.

I got right up to the tree. It smelled heavenly. I tucked the garden shears in my back pocket and put my ladder against the tree so I could clamber up to the lower branches to start climbing. Even back then I wasn't much of a climber, but I had a cause. *Snap!* The shears cut the first vine. It tumbled to the ground. *Snap!* A second vine was pruned and fell to the ground. *Snap, snap, snap!* More vines were cut and fell to the ground. It wasn't long before the base of the tree the vine grew on was a foot deep with cut vines and fragrant blossoms.

I thought, *I'll bet I even smell like flowers myself.* So I climbed down, gathered an armful of cut vines and headed home. It took me five trips to haul the ladder and all the vines and blossoms back to the house.

I was exhausted by then, but my job wasn't finished yet, so I set to work. My trusty ladder came in handy once more, leaning it up against a wall where I draped some paintings in trailing vines and blossoms. Then it was lampshades that got adorned. And windowsills and end tables were next to be festooned. I even had enough to put runners around the base of the walls. The whole living room smelled like a bottle of perfume—kind of like the perfume I bought at Perry's 5-and-10 for Mom on Mother's Day.

Sweet pungent garlands of blooms adorned everything I could reach with my ladder. I twirled in a slow circle to look at my handiwork—it was just perfect. Just right for our special friends. There was something beautiful and something that smelled sweet, but not cloying. Our friends would be so pleased with the effect. And Mom would be happy-surprised, too. I knew she had a great dinner planned. I could already smell the garlic and onions in the oven and I saw cookies cooling on the stovetop. (I didn't even snitch one.) Everything was going to be festive and special for our friends and my family to break bread together.

I was so exhausted that I took a nap; the only one I voluntarily took in my childhood. Mostly naps took cajoling and sometimes even exercises of parental authority. But this time I crawled into my bed all on my own. I was bushed! Worn out from the trek and the decorating.

I don't know how long I slept. But my dreams were rudely interrupted by a scream. "What's all this mess on the walls and floors and furniture? I spent hours getting the house clean—and now I'll have to do it all over again!"

I didn't hear all that. But what I did hear was the familiar summons. "Rick—y—y—y—y!" I'd been deep enough asleep not to hear anything but the trailing tone, "Rick-y-y!"

When I got into the living room, Mom was in tears, standing in the middle of the floor. Her hands were fluttering around up and down and sideways in futile gestures that indicated the work she had done—and needed to do again. I'd been expecting accolades for my ingenuity. But soon I joined her as I looked up at my handiwork. It was all drab, drooping and dead. The living room looked like an overgrown cemetery that hadn't been cared for in decades. The blooms had wilted, the vines had drooped. And the smell was like wet, damp dirt just after a heavy rain.

Needless to say, I vowed to myself never to cut another yellow jasmine again. To this day I enjoy them on people's back fences and in the woods. But I have yet to ever cut one.

After Mom had gotten over the initial shock, she sat down in the middle of the floor and pulled me gently onto her lap. From my sobs and tears, she could see there was no malicious intent. I'd only wanted to do what she was doing—making things special. Soothingly, she began to talk to me about how living things that are cut down don't live very long. She reminded me about the roses she'd cut from the garden and put in a vase, "They look pretty for a while, but after I pick them, they die. They get their food from the ground. And when they're cut, they don't have any way to get more plant food."

Then she began to talk about our dog, Specky Lou, who had just died. I'd remembered that sad day—how we'd dug a hole in the ground in the backyard, wrapped Specky Lou in her favorite *binky*, laid her into the ground and covered her up. "The flowers are like her," Mom had concluded. "The flowers looked healthy, climbing all over the tree, and they were, but their hold on life was fragile. They couldn't last long after they'd been cut."

I helped Mom take all the dead vines down from the places I'd painstakingly placed them. In great armfuls, we carted them out into the backyard. I remember digging a hole in the ground. It seemed so deep back then. Then I placed the vines in the hole, tamping them down with the shovel until they were all scrunched up in wads. And I covered them up—like we'd done with Specky Lou. I can still remember the solemn prayer I offered over them after I'd finished.

> Jesus said, *"I am the vine and you are the branches. Cut off from me you can do nothing."*
>
> John15:5 (Translation from *The Worshipbook)*

A Stable And A Star

I was feeling insignificant that day, as I sat there in my study with Christmas Eve service only hours away. The details of the season almost seemed to be enveloping me, dwarfing me into insignificance. I dialed up for the joy of Christmas and got a busy signal.

"The papers were piled on the desk without care in hopes that St. Nicholas soon would be there." No! That's not how Clemens wrote it; that's just how it felt.

I was feeling very insignificant that day, my single wish being to go back home and get lost in the bedcovers. Yes, I did feel that small. It was a day of *pouring over the carnage of the past* and realizing my fervent dreams and plans of youth were not going to happen. Maybe it's just me, but I suspect not.

When I'd looked ahead into my future with the hopeful, innocent eyes of an eighteen year old, I had been thrilled with the prospect. I wanted to burst through the years and be there, basking in the full glory I just knew would be mine.

But that was years ago, and now I was feeling very insignificant because I felt that I could never make my dreams happen. I had finally admitted to myself that the parade in my honor down Main Street of my hometown would never take place. Up until now, I had been sure that one day I'd walk into a room of childhood friends and they would push and shove to shake my hand, each one straining to help me remember their connection to me. And in the corners of the room, squeezed out by the crush, the rest of the people would be fumbling all over themselves to tell each other that they had sat next to me in second period history class, or had been the scene painter in a play I had starred in, or perhaps we had gone on a band trip together.

At seventeen, as I slipped out of high school anonymously for the last time, I made a solemn vow to myself that one day I'd return. And everyone would know. It would be an event of major proportions.

I was feeling very insignificant that day because I could see my solemn vow lying before me in tatters and shattered pieces.

A knock on the door interrupted my pall of disillusionment. The man who entered was tall, handsome and well dressed. I'd met him when he came to worship. I scrambled to gather the shattered pieces of my pain so I could see what he needed. I knew I would need to gather those pieces together; some shapeless pain in his eyes told me I'd need to.

He came into my office and crumpled into a chair. He had a craggy, chiseled jaw and I could almost see the chunks of granite in that jaw flake off and tumble to the floor. He'd hardly flopped down before he broke into deep, breath-stopping sobs. The wrenching waves were too deep even for tears, but I knew they too would come soon.

"*It's over! It's over!*" he moaned, rocking back and forth. There was nothing I could do or say right then, so I took his hand. He clutched my hand until I thought he would crush it.

After a time, the unvoiceable hurt began to subside and he looked up at me. "I came home. She and Cathy were gone! All they left was a note that said, *This time it's for good. Don't try to find us. We won't be there.* That's all she could say after six years of marriage," he cried.

I could see the crumpled note in his other hand. He told me how he'd torn through the house in disbelief. Clothes and toys were gone; he guessed the rest of it was inside those anonymous boxes labeled, *Will send for later.*

"I was on the way home and stopped to get a carton of cigarettes at the market where we always go," he said. "I wrote a check for them and a little left over for pocket money and they said there wasn't enough money in the account to cover the check."

"There had to be enough," he protested. "I deposited my Christmas bonus—$5,000—in the account the day before. I wondered what had happened at the bank, but thought I'd just check it out when they opened up after Christmas.

"It wasn't until I got the note that I finally worked out what was going on." He smashed the chair arm with his fist.

We talked for an hour or so. His story tumbled out in a jumble of hopes and dreams. As he began to wind down, I knew he was going to leave soon. And I wasn't ready for him to go. His sharing with me somehow made me feel significant, at least for a moment. I wasn't ready to feel insignificant again. I wanted my significance to last.

I locked the outside door behind him, and, for a moment, watched him walk away. I was pleased to see that he walked more erect than when he had come into this sacred haven hunched over and about to crumble.

I felt significant for a time, but it quickly ebbed and once again I felt insignificant. Briefly, I wondered if the man stood taller because he had left his own insignificance on me. Of course, I knew better. My insignificance was of my own doing, not his.

I was pondering the mercurial quality of my insignificance and significance when I happened to glance at the Nativity scene the children had made in Sunday School. At first I looked at the crude feeding trough where the baby lay. It was constructed with tongue depressors crossed and slatted, with straw poking over the top and through the cracks. What an insignificant place for the Son of God to be born.

Then my attention was grabbed by the whopper-jawed star covered in tinfoil.

Imagine, I thought and almost said out loud. *Imagine, that a star drew people from far away places to this significant, yet insignificant, place. The baby probably felt pretty insignificant that day, too. Maybe the visitors changed that feeling for a little while.*

Insignificance and Significance—Stable and Star. It's rather like my life!

Luke tells us, *"Mary gave birth to her first son, wrapped him in strips of cloth and laid him in the trough—there was no room for them to stay in the inn."*

Luke 2:7 (original translation)

Paul wrote to the Romans, "But now God's way of putting people right with himself has been revealed... God puts people right through their faith in Jesus Christ"

Romans 3: 21–2 (TEV)

Seeds Of Death And Life

The couple stood anxiously by the infant's hospital crib. From the fear furrows on their brows and the tear-reddened eyes, it was obvious the infant was theirs. Coffee stains blotched the father's sweat-stained shirt; at least one day's beard shadowed his face. The mother was covered by a flowered flannel nightgown with a forgotten price tag dangling from its neck. Beeps and whirrs of life-support monitors accompanied the regular wheeze of the respirator to create a hypnotic background chorus.

A nurse popped into the unit. "Michelle, you've simply got to go back to your room," she cajoled. "You'll endanger your own health if you don't. Doctor Patterson put you on strict bed rest for a good reason. We let you come down to neonatal for a quick visit—against orders—please..."

"In a minute." The mother couldn't seem to tear her eyes from the face of her long-awaited baby.

"All right, just a minute more—then back to bed with you.

"Jason," Nurse Cummings added, "you see that she does."

A vague nod acknowledged her order.

Little Matthew never really had a chance. He was so sick when he was born. No one had ever thought that a sterile, white space with insistent beepings and whirrings would be the result of nine months of waiting...and waiting...and waiting for this first-born to arrive.

When Doctor Patterson entered, the machines didn't skip a beat. She could tell from the monitors that nothing had changed; the only things keeping Matthew alive were the beeping, whirring machines. "The brain scan results are back," the doctor reported softly. "There's been no change. He could live on indefinitely or die at any moment, but he'll never have real life. He's brain dead."

"Not yet!" Matthew's mother sobbed, "Not yet!—too soon! Some miracle might happen."

The doctor could see Jason trying to console her when he himself was in need of consolation. He looked over at the doctor who slowly shook her head. Pain etched Dr. Patterson's face as she mouthed the words to Jason, "There's-no-hope."

Jason shuddered as he began to relate to Michelle what needed to happen, "Remember," he told her,

"Remember what they told us; that Matthew can give life to other babies?

With tears flowing,. the doctor guided the couple toward the power switches. They reached out slowly. Then, as one flesh, the turned the switches off. The lights began to go out, one after another. The monotonous hum of the flat-line told them what they'd all known, deep down inside. Matthew was dead. They turned out the lights and walked of the cubicle.

⌁

Hours later, in Seattle, the lights went on in the eyes of two anxious parents. They stood by the hospital crib of an infant. Little Julie was so pale she almost faded into the off-white bed linens. Julie needed a heart. Hers was malformed and could not function on its own for long. Her parents' life had been a roller coaster of hope and disappointment. They faced one crisis after another— each glimmer of light quickly dashed by another disappointment. Just hours before, they'd been told Julie had only a few hours of life left.

But suddenly the quiet room erupted. Dr. Craig rushed in to announce the good news. "A healthy heart has been found. It's on its way here by plane. We're taking Julie upstairs to surgery. The nurses will keep you updated. This will take hours. You two, get some rest! Little Julie's going to need you." They were jubilant.

Matthew's heart worked just fine.

⌁

Late that night, the light went on in the eyes of a single mother in Pittsburgh. She'd been silently weeping as she looked at Luke, her young son, who was strapped to the dialysis machine.

This is no life for a three-year-old, tied to this machine for hours at a time, she raged in silence. *He's had to spend more and more time doing this. It's unnatural for a child to lie that still.*

As the mother hovered over her child, she too got the message of light. Dr. Adams rushed in and the room erupted when he brought the news, "A kidney has been found! It's on its way."

Matthew's kidney allowed Luke to rise up and run.

<hr />

Early the next week, Eugenia opened her eyes. For the first time she knew what it meant to see. Her three years of life hadn't prepared her for this new sensation. All she'd ever known were blurs of light and dark. Now she knew what those blobs really looked like. In a tiny spasm of fear of the unknown, she shut her eyes tight.

"It's okay, honey," her father soothingly comforted. "Now you can know what we've been talking about."

She, too, would be able to see Jesus—because of little Matthew.

And Jesus said, "A seed remains no more than a single seed unless it's dropped into the ground and dies. If it does die, then it produces many seeds."

John 12:24 (paraphrased)

The Call

I sat there with my eyes glued to the bay window of my office. From it I could see a panorama of cars driving by or parking, and people entering for worship. I'd done all my preparations for Sunday worship. I'd read out loud my sermon manuscript so many times I could probably do it without the pages—but I knew I wouldn't.

I was looking for strange cars that might be coming for worship. A new Lincoln Town Car zipped into a parking place—maybe—no, Jack and Mary got out. It must be a new car. My watch continued—eyes moving back and forth.

It had been an exhausting week emotionally. I'd had four funerals. Each of them had become close friends during my 10-year stay at this lively congregation of older folks—over two-thirds of them widows and only a fraction under 70. I guess I should have expected it—all these funerals in a congregation with as many older people—but it had happened so often that I felt I buried a part of myself with each one. I needed to leave; find another congregation that would call me. I guess I loved these people too much.

I'd been runner-up several times. I made the final four in several very large congregations, but the fact that I'd spent so many years in a smaller congregation caused doubts in their minds about whether I was prepared to serve a congregation so large. One rejection letter from a church I'd contacted even said, "You're the best communicator we've found—far and away the best, but..."

So I was still pouring over activities I could see on the street.

Two strange cars turned the corner onto the church's street: a Buick Park Avenue and a Ford Crown Victoria. Both were full of people. Then my spirits soared when I saw out-of-state license plates. I knew it must be a pulpit committee coming to check me out. They got out of their cars and spread out, some waiting behind, so it wouldn't be so obvious.

I turned back to my desk for one last glimpse of my sermon and prayers. There beside the manuscript was the apology letter. I could feel the anger and insincerity flowing out of it. An associate executive of the regional office of my denomination had given—on purpose—some bad advice about a regional job fair. I'd followed it, and the result was to my detriment. It made it difficult for me to attend future ones. I'd written to her superior about what had happened. Apparently she got called on the carpet for it and the letter was supposed to make amends. But I could tell it was forced. I blocked that memory from my mind and began the usual prayers I offered alone in my office for God to speak through me.

With an ebullient spirit, I entered the sanctuary with the choir. I could see the strangers spread out over the congregation, but astute members of my congregation wouldn't be fooled—another pulpit committee.

The sermon I'd prepared was a good one in my estimation, even though it was a little different from the typical sermon most of my colleagues would have used. I was speaking about the prophesy from Isaiah about the Messiah who would bring good news to the poor, heal the broken-hearted, release the captives and prisoners and proclaim a time when the Lord would save the people. It was the very passage Jesus read in the synagogue in his hometown that got him in so much hot water because he announced the prophecy was fulfilled in him. What made the sermon different were brief vignettes that would help the audience emotionally identify with the people affected by the *Day of the Lord*.

As the sermon progressed I sensed that I had everyone in the palm of my hand as I described the victory to come. It was more than just preparation, though, my previous work had placed me in good stead. I was able to make eye contact with the listen-

ers with only an occasional glance down to my manuscript. And then the worship was over.

I was still *flying high* as the people greeted me at
the front door. As usual I hugged many of them, particularly the women who were all alone after decades
with their life companion. Several people commented
on the content of the sermon and how it had moved
them. The strangers mixed in with those leaving.
Finally only one man remained in the sanctuary. He
came up to me and asked if *they* could take my wife
and me out to lunch. I tried to dampen my excitement some and readily agreed. I guess Barbara, my
wife, had noticed the gaggle of strangers, so she was
standing nearby. She winked and nodded acceptance,
and I accepted the invitation for us.

The luncheon was a complete success. For more
than two hours we fielded questions. One asked about
my ministerial weaknesses. After a moment, I decided
to tell them the truth: I needed help in administration details. They told us about the congregation. It
was only then that I realized we were visiting with the
committee from a large congregation in the capitol
city of a nearby state. It had a history dating back to
the earliest settlement of the state while it was still
only a territory. I had to keep my mouth from dropping open in awe. I glanced at Barbara and noticed her
quiet stifling of surprise. After we'd talked for a long
time, they asked us to leave the private room they'd
reserved in one of the nicest restaurants in the city. It
was only moments later, but seemed like an eternity,

before the man who'd extended the luncheon invitation asked us to rejoin them.

He asked if we could fly up to their city in the near future. One woman blurted out, "As near in the future as possible." She blushed at her minor indiscretion. My day off was on a Friday, so that gave us from Thursday evening through Saturday. I mentioned that and each nodded excitedly. By now I'd realized the man who'd spoken to me was the chairman of the committee. "The tickets will be waiting for you at the airport."

The ensuing week dragged by until the time of departure finally arrived. We both felt like a village of butterflies had taken residence in our bodies. We arrived just on time. There was little baggage to be dealt with, so our departure was easy.

The head of the committee greeted us as we picked up our bags and drove us into the city, directly to the church. My mouth did flop open when I saw it. It was a towering Gothic structure with attached buildings that seemed to go on and on. The rest of the committee greeted us at the church along with several other ladies not on the committee. The latter group invited Barbara for a tour of the city. Later on, I found out that two of them were realtors. Barbara said they zipped past the scenic attractions and seemed to be concentrating on the housing neighborhoods.

Meanwhile I talked some more with the committee—a few questions that hadn't been dealt with previously. Then they gave me a tour of the church, saving the sanctuary for last. The buildings were old, but well-kept and modernized. They talked about some of the things they did for mission, including feeding the homeless once a day, every day. A woman in the committee chimed in, "Some of our folks weren't too keen about the ragtag group they encountered coming for Sunday School, but they were reminded of the importance of the mission and acquiesced. We then asked the homeless group to stick around the kitchen area where they wouldn't be so conspicuous."

As we entered the sanctuary I felt my eyes being lifted up by the soaring nature of the room. There were biblical stained glass windows all around and in between were tall columns that reached up to the ceiling. The plan was a sort of V-shape, focusing in on the pulpit. I felt a kind of humbling sensation at the responsibility that would be placed on me. I'd seen the gallery of former ministers. Many of them I'd heard of, even read some of their writings in seminary. The committee chairman asked if I wanted to stand in the pulpit. I could tell this was more than just an invitation. But, in true Southern gentility, it was offered as an option. I had to walk up a set of narrow stairs. It was then that I began to notice the ornate woodwork that filled the sanctuary. When I got to the top, I saw the sounding board overhead intended to project speech before the days of microphones. I whispered something to myself, then was embarrassed because it could be heard in every spot in the big room. I then noticed there still were no microphones. I glanced down at the pulpit itself and saw a narrow slab of aged marble with the simple text: *Sir, we would see Jesus.* I felt like I wanted to stay there forever. A voice broke my reverie, "We need to meet with the Board. They've come here for a special meeting to check you out."

The boardroom had the dark-wooded look of an English Library, except for the free-form walnut conference table in the center surrounded by comfortable cushioned chairs. The first ones to enter had an austere, solemn look about them. To a man—yes, man—they were dressed in dark suits with conservative ties. Then a number of women entered. They were fashionably dressed and added the only color to the gathered assemblage. The committee chairman introduced me. A few questions were asked, but they seemed perfunctory. As I talked I noticed that their eyes were fixed on me. It might have been my imagination, but when the interview was concluded, I thought I noticed faint smile lines in many of their somber faces.

The rest of the weekend was a whirl of activity. They took me over to the state capitol complex, and I was introduced to a number of senators and representatives who regularly attended church while they were in session. Then I was introduced to the governor of the state. He was a handsome. For a few minutes he regaled me with stories about sermons he'd heard at the church, even some which tromped on his toes a little. Jokingly, he stated, "I hope that you'll realize that I have bunions, and it's painful when a preacher tromps on my toes."

Saturday noon came. Barbara and I were taken to

a private dinner club atop one of the city skyscrapers for an elegant lunch. All the committee members were there. "We're kind of bleary-eyed," the chairman announced, "We were up pretty late last night after we'd sent you all back to the hotel. It will be our recommendation to the congregation that they call you as our senior pastor, beginning at your earliest convenience."

In excitement Barbara and I *high-fived* each other.

"I guess," said the chairman with a broad smile, "that we have your answer."

"You sure do!" both of us said at once.

Back to a more serious tone, the chairman said," Of course, we'll have to have you examined by the regional committee for ministers. They can see you two weekends from now. Is that agreeable?"

I nodded, "I'll need at least two months to do a good job of saying good-bye to my present congregation. We've spent quite a few years together and I don't feel I can just up and leave without some preparation and helping them get their transition process started.

A couple members frowned, but one woman, who'd not said a word during the whole time stated, "I'd expect that from a good pastor. We're anxious for you to be here, but it's only right that your good-byes be done right." Then the few with frowns nodded their agreement. We did some planning about when to call the congregational meeting to extend the call and when my first Sunday would be. They said the church owned an apartment we could use in the transition between selling our house and finding the right one for us.

"Well," announced the chairman, "I'd better get you back to the airport, but I want to see if you can meet one woman in our church who's into a lot of things. I've tried calling her, but she hasn't answered." He pulled out a cell phone and tried calling her once more—unsuccessfully. Then he called someone else and found out that she was away on a cruise and wouldn't be back for a month.

"I'm sorry you can't meet her," he said. "She's got lots of barbs on the outside, but a good heart underneath. I'd hoped you and she could get together when you came back for the examination, but I guess that can't happen.

"One thing I haven't said, but, in all fairness, I need to say. The departure of our previous minister wasn't a happy one. He was involved in a few things... but let's not get into those details. They aren't important. I guess I want to say we want to be sure about who follows him and we unanimously agree that you'll fit the bill quite nicely."

Two weeks later, the examination with the regional committee went off well. I was thrown several *knuckleball* questions and fielded them quite well. After those questions, the rest of the meeting was almost a *love fest*.

Back home, Barbara and I were bursting with

excitement and frustrated that we couldn't tell anybody. So privately we jumped up and down with joy.

A week before the congregational meeting was to
be held, we were watching television. The phone rang.
It was the chairman of the committee. Immediately
I noticed a hesitant sadness in his voice. "A problem
has come up. There's been some new information,
and I'm sorry to say the congregational vote will be a
significantly divided one. Your call will be approved,
but there'll be a lot of opposition to deal with if you
decide to come."

In anguish I asked, "What's being said? Maybe I
can answer some of the questions. Please tell me."

"Unfortunately, I'm not at liberty to discuss the
matter because of confidences I've agreed upon. But
you're still welcome to try."

I read between the lines quite clearly—he didn't
want to face the fight that would ensue. It was clear
to me that after a questionable departure of the previous minister, that a divided call would not be a good
idea.

With tears in my voice, I choked out, "I guess we'd
better end things here. I had felt like there was much
I could do with your congregation. In my excitement
I've already made some plans. I'll send them to you.
They're in rough form, but I think they might help
the one you ultimately choose to be your minister."

I could hear the catch in his voice. "That's mighty
fine of you, considering the way you're being treated.
I hadn't intended to tell you, but, to a person, the

committee feels like you should be our minister. In fact, one member of the committee has already made it plain she's leaving the church because of the way you were treated." The catch in his voice became more obvious as he cleared his throat to cover it. "I'm seriously thinking of doing so myself. I've been in this church for all my life, but it will be hard for me to swallow what's happened."

We said our good-byes. A primal scream erupted from my mouth. I doubled over in pain and ran to the spare bedroom, still screaming, mixed with crying. Barbara had been in the kitchen making popcorn during the brief phone conversation, so she didn't know what had happened. She hugged me and rocked me and finally got out of me that the call wasn't to be.

After a couple months, the worst of the pain and disappointment began to pass. I called the regional executive in that district. He said he didn't know what happened. But I sensed there was more he could have told me.

One Year Later

I have a friend in one of my pastimes that I'd shared my heartache with. He said, "That's horribly unfair. I know a guy up there that's got a lot of connections among people *in the know* in that congregation. I'll see if he can find out what happened."

A month later he called me. "You got shafted. Some executive here in our area phoned a woman with clout in that congregation, and here's the gist of what I heard.–

——You'd end their ministry to street people.

—You'd taken a going church and killed it.

—You're all talk and no do.

—And the folks in your congregation really wanted you gone."

I was stunned into silence. "Hey, you still there, friend?" my confidante asked.

I croaked out a yes, then got very angry. "All that's *bull!* First, I've been an on-going advocate for the poor and have involved my congregation in lots of programs in the projects near the church.

"Second, this congregation was considering closing its doors when I came here. I was kind of a one last chance. And we've grown. New couples are starting to join and be quite active. We were pulling off the almost impossible—skipping two generations to draw in folks that are the age of these folks' grandchildren.

"Third, I've been pumping life into this congregation the whole time I've been here. The fact that young couples are joining comes directly from my initiative.

"Fourth—savvy folks here recognized that pulpit committee. I can't tell you how many of them have said to me privately, "I hope you don't leave us. We need you.

"It's a crock of lies, and I think I know who started them."

The next week I got up the nerve to go to the regional office. Several secretaries got up from their work to give me a hug. And the one who dealt with relations with ministers said to me with a tear in her eye, "I know. I can't say anything else, but I know."

When I got to the next level, I received condolences, but was stonewalled when I asked for details. But the details became quite clear when the associate I'd had a run-in with smirked as she saw me.

Seven Years Later

After a long struggle with illness that was just beginning when the magic call vanished, my wife died. I was headed to North Carolina for her burial. I felt I needed some support. So I stopped along the way to visit with people who'd been special to me: the girl I'd dated in college, the campus minister from my college days. My last stop was to visit a tall steeple colleague who'd been a very good friend when we served in the same city.

He'd just got a call to an enormous, prestigious, old historical congregation that was over 200 years old. I walked around and around the building before I spotted the office entrance. It was locked, and I had to be buzzed in. A solemn receptionist took one look at my traveling attire and asked what my business was. I said I wanted to visit my friend who'd just been called there as a minister. She replied that she didn't think he was holding office hours and could I come back two days later. I was getting a little huffy by now. "Just check with him and see if he wants to see me."

With some disdain she punched in some numbers on the phone. After three conversations (I expected with secretaries), she announced that he might spare a few minutes. It was obvious to me she couldn't understand why he'd want to see such a disheveled man as me. Then it got to the directions. She said she'd better write them down. This floored me, but I was soon grateful she had. I wandered around the cavernous building until I found a narrow set of stairs that she'd indicated would lead to his office. Up the stairs I went. I knocked on the door, but no response. Then I noticed a doorbell. I couldn't figure out why a doorbell was needed inside a building, but I pressed it.

Immediately my friend came bounding through the door to usher me into the office. It was a Chippendale and English library office. There was a freeway right nearby, but I couldn't hear a single sound from it. My friend latched onto my hand.

"I needed to see a friendly face. I'm bottled up in this soundproof office all day and hardly see a single human being." His greeting was so effusive I could sense he really needed to see me.

I told him I was on the way to bury Barbara. He came around from his desk and enveloped me in his arms. After a while he offered a prayer of condolence for me. "I never get to do that kind of thing anymore," he said longingly. "I've been put on such a pedestal here nobody talks one-on-one—you know, just friendly conversation, even a gross joke or two."

I stayed for more than an hour and realized I needed to get going. I'd be late getting to Barbara's family as it was. I said I needed to go, and he kept asking me to stay longer. Finally I really did need to leave and he looked so disappointed it broke my heart.

I descended the steps, and wandered around the building, not finding where I'd come in. Finally I found an outside door and left. As I was driving down the freeway, listening to a book on tape, a lightning bolt thought almost made me stop in the middle of the freeway. I found a rest area and pulled in to find out what I was telling myself.

The vision I had brought tears of relief. I saw myself at state capitol First Church, remembering the aerie that would have been my office. Someone would have had to go through two sets of secretaries and quite a walk to have gotten to me.

Even though I know the right thing happened, the injustice of it ate away at me for years. I knew I had to let it go somehow. So on the anniversary of the rejection phone call, I wrote a letter of forgiveness to the woman who'd been so unjust to me. I guess I'll never know how she reacted because I never got a reply.

You know, God, You sure do know your people, don't you? I'd have starved at that church I was so heartbroken I didn't get to go to. *Thanks!*

And Paul writes: We know that in all things God works for good with those who love God.

Romans 8:28 (TEV)

Visions Of God's Kingdom

Several years ago, I took a trip to Epcot Center. One of the pavilions I visited featured a 360-degree, multiscreen movie about China. There was a swatch of a picture here and another there. Sometimes five or six going at once. Isaiah 11: 1–9 is rather like that movie presentation. It's a dazzling set of visions giving glimpses of the kind of world God has in store for us. And what a world it will be!

A small green shoot sprouting up from a tree stump. The ultimate leader: one who governs with fairness and justice and integrity! Wolves living together with sheep! Calves and lion cubs having lunch together! A baby playing near a rattlesnake! It will be a world where there will be nothing harmful or bad—a world filled to overflowing with the knowledge of God and God's ways.

When election time looms, we citizens see candidates jockeying for position, scrabbling and backbiting over who'll lead our nation, none of them displaying much leadership. We hear candidate promises, ones we suspect will never be kept. We look to Israel and get our hopes raised, only to have them dashed and raised again in a roller coaster powered by centuries-old grievances. We see the volatility of North Korea and other dictator-led countries. And then there's crime that invades even the most protected places. We watched on television screens as terrorists strike where we'd thought we'd be safe. And it makes us wonder where the next target might be. Here? Our city?

With all this, Isaiah's vision is a portrait for us to absorb. It allows us to see one after another of the beautiful, hopeful visions of what God has in store when Jesus comes again. Isaiah's prophetic vision tells us about the world God's going to make out of the chaos and meanness we've created.

But before we get all wrapped up in the fantastic happenings, part of understanding that vision involves looking at the context of the words. The people who heard them were in a pretty tough spot. Removed from all that was familiar, they were a beaten people, a disillusioned people, a people vulnerable to the whims of others, a people having to scrap and scrape just to get by—the exiled Jews in Babylon. They'd been forcibly wrenched out of their homes and put in what would now be modern-day Iraq—an impossible journey from all that was familiar to them. And they were made to live at the beck and call of the people who'd leveled their capitol city to the ground.

To fully feel the joy of Isaiah's vision, we need to experience what the Exile feels like. We have many exiles in our own world. There are many today who aren't too different from those who first heard the good news of the Messiah being proclaimed. For them our celebration of Christ's birth isn't a happy time.

～

For instance, Jane, whose husband didn't come home one night last July. She scrounged a job. But after rent, utilities, food and the basics, there was nothing left to make Christmas for her four children. As she sits in front of the TV, each commercial makes her madder, sadder, more frustrated. "For that someone special," she hears, "designer jeans—because you're worth it. A Mercedes Benz—starting under $30,000. A Keepsake diamond. And for the children on your list—the latest doll, newest electronic game, a top-of-the-heap skateboard, hundred dollar sneakers—all things kids think they need to belong to the *in* crowd. Jane's mind wanders to the closet that's off limits to the kids and thinks of its meager contents—warm jackets for Richard and Jimmy, things they have to have. Her stomach grumbles remembering the lunches she skipped to buy them. There are shoes for Suzy and Rachel—she's put cardboard insoles in theirs for so long they bow out when it rains. A tear rolls down Jane's cheek. She slams off the TV and goes to her room for a good cry—the third this week.

And then there's Miss Amanda. She's sitting in her living room, surrounded by chintz, horsehair covers, shades drawn and a clutter of mementos from her 85 years of life. Last week she buried her last sibling. There'd been ten once. Now only Miss Amanda. The space heater works overtime to warm the chill winds that seep through the cracks in the old house. Miss Amanda thinks about the nativity scene her grandfather carved. It had been her custom each year to go into the attic to get it. Then she'd carefully dust each figure and arrange them on the dining room table. *It's not worth it this year,* she sighs. *There's no one to see it.*

James William Harriman Roosevelt, IV is sitting at the conference table in Geneva. The disarmament talks have broken down again. He wonders to himself if they'll do any good even if they start up again. His stomach knots at the horror of a nuclear war. He knows better than most just what could happen by the simple touch of a finger.

Visions of exile, of loneliness, of fear, of anger—pictures of the world the people faced who heard Isaiah's prophesy. These visions of defeat aren't difficult for us to conjure up. In the midst of our celebrations, we know that, beneath the tinsel and wrapping paper of Christmas is a world in desperate need of God's change.

What a world that would be! What images could Isaiah bring to us that we'd readily comprehend?

Let's disengage our brains for a minute. Let's listen to these pictures with our hearts. Let's hear and feel the good news God has in store for us.

Isaiah writes: *A shoot springs from the stump of Jesse's tree* (Isaiah 11:1). How can we understand that? Listen with your heart.

⁓

Mary Ann comes in from Christmas shopping, dumps a load of packages on the floor and happens to glance over at her plants. She's been pampering a particular plant for months, but it's been looking brown and brittle, its leaves drooping and dropping. She's been seriously thinking of giving up on this one. Then her eye catches something new—a small lump of green on the top of the stalk. "A new leaf is sprouting," she says out loud. Suddenly she isn't tired anymore. Isaiah's good news is kind of like that when we hear it with our hearts. And there's more.

⁓

Listen to the kind of leadership God's going to bring—the kind of people who'll be calling the shots in God's world. Isaiah promises us, *On him the spirit of the Lord rests, a spirit of wisdom and insight, a spirit of counsel and power, a spirit of knowledge and the fear of the Lord. The fear of the Lord is his breath. He doesn't judge by appearances. He gives no verdict on hearsay, but judges the wretched with integrity, and with equity gives a verdict for the poor of the land. His word is a rod that strikes the ruthless; his sentences bring death to the wicked. Integrity is the loincloth round his waist* (11:2–5).

∽

I don't know about you, but I'm not very impressed with what I see and hear during election times. I fear that I've grown jaundiced and cynical because I've heard all the promises before, yet nobody has fulfilled them. And we people are a major part of the political illness of our land. We want to be entertained instead of informed, so we can make a decision. We want leaders who make decisions based on what benefits *me* and not on what's right. We pooh-pooh politicians and the news media, but they are our own creations.

Fantasize with me the kind of government that God's government will bring. A candidate whose breath is—the fear of the Lord. A leader whose decisions are based on the word of God instead of political give and take, this influence peddler or that voting block. A person who gets a law passed that is the same for all people, not for expediency, but because it's right.

To continue with our heart-trip, Isaiah draws us a picture of a world reconciled, where natural enemies live side-by-side in peace. He tells us that *the wolf lives with the lamb, the panther laid down with the kid, calf and lion cub feed together with a little boy to lead them. The cow and the bear make friends, their young lie*

down together. The lion eats straw like the ox, the infant
plays over the cobra's hole; into the snake's lair the young
child puts his hand. They do no hurt, no harm on all my
holy mountain. (11:6–9a).

The words from Isaiah have a richness about them.
In my heart's eye I see a

joyous, jumbled painting. On the upper right, I
watch the Texas A&M offensive line throwing blocks
for a running back from University of Texas. On the
upper left, I see Ralph Nader and refinery managers
working together to find ways to clean our air at a
reasonable cost. In the lower left I see Ted Kennedy
consulting Tom DeLay to create a piece of legisla-
tion. In the lower right I see U.S. and Iraqi citizens
volunteering to rebuild wrecked cities with U.N. representatives overseeing their efforts. Off to one side
I see nations of the world agreeing to end, not just
some nuclear arms, but everything that goes bang and
kills people. I see George Wallace and Martin Luther
King building a playground for children of all colors
and shapes. Of to the other side, I see Jesse Jackson
and a Klansman serving meals on wheels to blacks
and whites and having a good time with each other.
I see Presbyterians of all different persuasions working together to find solutions instead of just staking
out their turf. And right smack dab in the middle of
the phantasmagorical painting I see a campfire. Pales-
tinians and Israelis are dancing side by side. Leaders
from Lebanon, Syria, Iran, Iraq, Saudi Arabia, Cuba,
African nations, Al Qaeda and other terrorist factions,

as well as North and South Korea, Pakistan, India, Russia, China, and the United States are arm-in-arm dancing around the campfire like the cast did in the movie, Zorba the Greek.

Below that I see politicians throwing ballots up in the air like confetti and joining together to lead our land. I see the killer of Matthew Shepherd and his mother working on a Wyoming roadside park at the spot where Matthew's killing took place. And I see Klansmen and the survivors of the James Byrd family digging and watering together, planting a forest of trees that will surround the Jasper courthouse and give shade for anyone who needs to sit in a cool spot for a minute.

This bizarre painting can become real when the knowledge of God becomes the determining factor. Special interests, warfare, centuries of grudges and intrigue can be washed away.

We probably will have to endure many things before that marvelous world comes about—or maybe not. But we can be confident that Emmanuel—God with us—will be there for us.

We who have walked in darkness now see a great light. On us who have lived in a land of shadow, a light has shown. Please share with me the vision of him who was born in a stable. Participate with me in ways to help usher in that marvelous kingdom.

Believe the good news: Emmanuel, God with us, will lead the way. Follow the One who will come in the name of the Lord.

The Lord says, "The time is coming when I will make a new covenant with the people of Israel and with the people of Judah...I will put my law within them and write it on their hearts."

Jeremiah 31: 3 (TEV)

The royal line of David is like a tree that been cut down; but just as new branches sprout from a stump, so a new king will arise from among David's descendants. The spirit of God will give him wisdom and the knowledge and skill to rule the people. The Messiah will know God's will and will have reverence for him, and find pleasure in obeying him. The Messiah will not judge by appearance or hearsay; he will judge the poor fairly and defend the rights of the helpless...He will rule the people with justice and integrity.

Wolves and sheep will live together in peace, and leopards will lie down with young goats. Calves and lion cubs will feed together and little children will take care of them. Cows and bears will eat together and their calves and cubs will lie down in peace. Lions will eat straw as cattle do. Even a baby will not be harmed if it plays near a poisonous snake.

On Zion, God's holy hill, there will be nothing harmful or evil. The land will be as full of the knowledge of God as the seas are full of water.

Isaiah 11:1–9 (TEV)

e|LIVE

---

listen|imagine|view|experience

AUDIO BOOK DOWNLOAD INCLUDED WITH THIS BOOK!

In your hands you hold a complete digital entertainment package. Besides purchasing the paper version of this book, this book includes a free download of the audio version of this book. Simply use the code listed below when visiting our website. Once downloaded to your computer, you can listen to the book through your computer's speakers, burn it to an audio CD or save the file to your portable music device (such as Apple's popular iPod) and listen on the go!

How to get your free audio book digital download:

1. Visit www.tatepublishing.com and click on the e|LIVE logo on the home page.
2. Enter the following coupon code:
   500e-9896-d5e1-6b4c-4016-43fc-5c0a-5c94
3. Download the audio book from your e|LIVE digital locker and begin enjoying your new digital entertainment package today!